UMBRA - SPECIAL EXTENDED EDITION

BOOK TWO OF THE DIMENSION DRIFT

CHRISTINA BAUER

COPYRIGHT

Monster House Books
Brighton, MA 02135
ISBN 9781945723674
First Edition

CONTENTS

DEDICATION

For All Those Who Kick Ass,
Take Names And Read Books

COLLECTED WORKS

Dimension Drift
Dystopian adventures with science, snark, and hot aliens
1. Scythe
2. Umbra
3. Alien Minds
4. ECHO Academy
5. Justice
6. Slate

Angelbound Origins
About a quasi (part demon and part human) girl who loves kicking butt in Purgatory's Arena
1. Angelbound
2. Scala
3. Acca
4. Thrax
5. The Dark Lands
6. The Brutal Time
7. Armageddon
8. Quasi Redux
9. Clockwork Igni
10. Lady Reaper

Angelbound Offspring
The next generation takes on Heaven, Hell, and everything in between
1. Maxon

2. Portia
3. Zinnia
4. Rhodes
5. Kaps
6. Mack
7. Huntress

Angelbound Lincoln

The Angelbound experience as told by Prince Lincoln

1. Duty Bound
2. Lincoln
3. Trickster
4. Baculum
5. Angelfire

Fairy Tales of the Magicorum

Modern fairy tales with sass, action, and romance

1. Wolves and Roses
2. Moonlight and Midtown
3. Shifters and Glyphs
4. Slippers and Thieves
5. Bandits and Ball Gowns
6. Fairies and Frosting

Pixieland Diaries

Sassy pixie Calla loves elf prince Dare. Too bad he hasn't noticed her. Yet.

1. Pixieland Diaries
2. Calla
3. Dare
4. Winter Prince
5. Ley Queen

Beholder

Where a medieval farm girl discovers necromancy and true love

1. Cursed
2. Concealed
3. Cherished
4. Crowned
5. Cradled
This is a completed series.

UMBRA

CHAPTER 1

"*Wish to travel the omniverse? First try leaping off a hovercraft without a power chute. Should you live, then you might survive in alternate realities as well.*" – Beauregard the Great, *Instructions for Visiting Parallel Worlds*

NINE MINUTES.

That's how long before this planet implodes.

I'm talking about a version of Earth that supports thousands of cities. Millions of buildings. Billions of people. Not to mention what's almost beyond counting. Like photographs. Sunflowers. Bowling trophies. Baby carriages. As of this moment, I'm the only barrier between all that and instant annihilation.

Welcome to my Tuesday.

I'm Thorne Oxblood, and I fight inter-dimensional disasters.

For my current mission, I'm at placelet 92.248.908, planet X3894-B, strand BT704.35, and branch point 1T.783-50E. The locals have a simpler name for this location, though. *Clyde's Gym.* Over the last hour, I've memorized every inch of this space, searching for the *schism*—meaning the inter-dimensional breaking point—that could tear this world apart. Nothing has shown itself yet. Nervous energy corkscrews up my shoulders and neck. *What am I missing?* For the umpteenth time, I inspect the gym.

Large, square space with concrete walls? *Check.*

Rickety slats in a worn-out floor? *Check.*

Faded girly calendars everywhere? *Odd decoration, but it's not my gym. And check.*

Points of access? *Three.* Main entrance up-front, an office side door, and a small emergency exit along the back wall. Since I arrived, no one's entered or left.

Huge letter K glowing on the ceiling? *Check.* This is something only I can see, and it means my family's arch-enemy, the Komandir, stopped by this gym at some point. Not as helpful a fact as one might think. It still doesn't show me where the schism is hiding.

Humans? *Nine.* Two boxers pound away in the sparring ring. Another six guys slam into punching bags, lift weights or jump rope. One teenage girl scribbles on papers behind the door marked *office*. Then, there's me. To the humans, I'm just an eighteen-year-old in gray sweats. Nothing about my muscular build, short hair, and blue eyes screams, *this guy's an alien.*

But I am from another world. *Umbra.*

And as an Umbran, my body stores tiny cybernetic organisms called sentient. These minute creatures enable me to guard the omniverse, which is the universe of universes. Tonight's mission marks my seventy-first rescue. For the record, my sentient are extra jacked up at this point. They keep sending me mental images of this planet exploding in a silent shower of blinding light.

Not for the first time, I try to calm them. *I got it,* I whisper in my mind. *There's trouble at Clyde's Gym.*

Another explosion image follows. *Not helping.*

I rub my temples and try to focus. *Think through the problem, Thorne.* Since I saw the glowing K, I've assumed the Komandir are behind the trouble here. But maybe the symbol is a distraction. Perhaps something else is at work. After all, these humans could be about to develop drift science, which is the ability to open alternate realities. Once you can visit other worlds, it's easier to implode your own. Drift science would also explain why my sentient keep sending images of exploding planets instead of pics showing Doc Zykin, the Komandir assassin.

Closing my eyes, I reach out to my sentient. *Is drift science the real problem here?*

In reply, my sentient show me beauty queens jumping up and down after winning a pageant. It's their way of saying, *yes already.* Amazing how, even though they can't speak, my sentient still manage to be sarcastic.

Fresh scenes flood my mind. This time, my sentient review my last mission.

I stand in a huge white space. A sign for New Cosmos University hangs above me; equipment covers the floor all around. There are tall monoliths with computer arrays, a patchwork of workstations, and round databots that zoom through the air. I stand at the drift science station, dressed in a white lab coat. It took me two weeks to infiltrate this place as a research student. After that, I spent days hacking into university systems so anyone with Umbran DNA would be immune to security. Yet the real time-suck on this mission has been my target, Helen Robbins. She's whip-smart with long black hair, cocoa skin, and a gaze that could melt titanium.

She thinks I'm up to something.

She's right.

Trouble is, my secret agenda is to stop this version of Earth from imploding. For that to happen, Helen must ace her latest set of drift science calculations. How do I know her calcs are key? My sentient keep making her data pad glow red. For weeks, I've tried to help her, but she keeps blocking any attempts at conversation. My only chance is that the school board wants fresh numbers today.

"How's it going?" I ask. "I know you're on a deadline."

Helen presses her tablet against her chest. "What's it to you?"

"I want to help. That's it. Honestly."

Helen pauses. Little by little, she starts handing me her datapad.

At last.

I could cheer.

Behind me, the lab door thuds open. My brother Justice bursts into the room. He's a bulky figure dressed in cowboy boots, a black T-shirt, jeans and a Stetson. In some kind of nod to science, he holds a pocket protector in his left hand. He stomps over to my side.

"How's it going, little bro?" Justice closes his eyes. I know what he's doing—accessing his sentient. "Guess you met the smartest filly in this here lab." Justice increases intensity as he says 'smartest filly.' I get it. Justice means that his sentient pinpointed Helen as the target for this mission. Sadly, my brother already has a loud and gravelly voice. Upping the volume only makes the words 'smartest filly' boom through the chamber. Everyone stops working to stare.

My jaw muscles lock in frustration. Justice came here to check on me, clear and simple. Did it take me a few days to determine Helen was my target? Sure. I don't have Justice's power over sentient, so I figured it out on my own. Now, I'm finally finishing my work here, and my brother shows up to 'help.'

He could ruin everything.

I look to Helen. She's clasped the datapad so tightly against her torso, the girl's knuckles flare white. "That's your brother?" she asks, her face scrunched in disbelief.

I pinch the bridge of my nose. "Yup. Can you ignore him?"

"I don't know." Helen takes a half-step backward. "He's really really really big."

Justice tips the brim of his Stetson. "Thank you, sugar."

"Wasn't a complement," deadpans Helen. Justice keeps right on smiling. He's convinced every woman loves him. Mostly because he's the most eligible bachelor on Umbra.

I step closer to Helen. "Please. You only deal with him once. I've got him for the rest of my life."

Helen pauses, then cracks a smile. "I've an older sister, too. Name's Polly." She hands over the datapad. "Poll's a lot like your brother."

"Is that right, now?" Justice flashes Helen a thousand-watt smile. "Is this Polly of yours all charm and sunshine, just like me?"

Helen chuckles. "Nope, she's more of a busybody. Thinks I can't do anything without her."

"So." Justice puffs out his lower lip. "Not like me."

While Helen and Justice chat, I scan the datapad, make a few notes, and hand it back. "Your results from the dark matter tests are off," I explain. The data comes another team, and I'm not surprised their work sucks. That group's more interested in clubbing than science. "Rerun the tests yourself and your calcs will be fine."

Helen scans the screen. "Thanks. If these numbers were off, it could have caused an explosion."

"Through space and time," adds Justice.

"Thanks," I tell my brother. "But I'm handling this." Which in family-speak translates to: shut the hell up.

Helen gives me the side eye. "How could you know those tests looked wrong? This is all new. No one's seen proper results yet."

Justice taps his temple. "My little brother here's a thinker. He's got to be, considering how he's low on sentient and all." Justice closes his eyes for a moment. "Good news. Now those numbers are put to rights, this here universe is safe again. Nice how things work out, huh?"

Helen frowns. "Did you say sentient?"

"Yes indeedy," replies Justice. My brother then turns to me. "Speaking of sentient, did you catch how mine said our work here is done? We aced this mission together, little bro."

"I caught that part, yes." I'd add that Justice did no actual work to ace said mission, but that will only lead to more humiliating speeches about my weakness with sentient.

Justice slaps his hand on my shoulder. "Let's get back to Umbra."

Helen's brows lift. "Umbra?"

I shake my head. "Oh, it's definitely time to leave."

The memory replay ends. It's obvious why my sentient showed me that scene. In Helen's world, fixing drift science was the key to saving her planet. The same could be true here as well. Even so, Helen's mission lasted for weeks and took place in a laboratory. This time, I've only got eight more minutes and a gymnasium.

Not gonna lie.

I'm at a loss here.

The main door swings open; five teenage guys step inside. All of them sport pomade-slick hair, white T-shirts, and cuffed jeans. *Classic greasers.* Which makes sense. After all, this parallel Earth broke off from the prime reality sometime in the 1950's. Branch worlds often get stuck on their exit point.

The tallest in the group pauses just inside the door. He's got a square face, a flat nose, and a great swoosh of blond hair. His stocky body seems ready to burst from his leather bomber jacket. A smaller teen pulls at the tall guy's elbow.

"Axel," he begins.

"Quiet, Runt."

"The name's Ralph," squeaks the little guy.

"You're whatever I call you." Axel elbows the smaller kid in gut. Ralph gasps in pain, but he doesn't fight back. *Interesting.* So whatever this group is, Axel is both their leader and a total dick. Not good. Axel's beady eyes narrow as he inspects the room.

He's looking for someone.

Beep... beep...

My earpiece lets out a soft tone that only I can hear. Based on the rhythm, I already know who's calling. *Justice.*

"Accept inbound comm," I say.

My brother's gravelly voice echoes across the line. "You've got less than seven minutes left, little brother. Vamoose."

"Not an option," I declare. "My mission isn't over."

"Then I'm coming after you. Now."

Right. Justice would be here already if I hadn't hidden my placelet data. After the disaster with Helen, I figured out that trick.

"Any news for me?" I ask.

"The S-Man got us some info."

By S-Man, Justice means Slate, our youngest brother. Together, the three of us make up the royal family for Umbra. As Emperor of the Omniverse, our father Cole wields the all-powerful Crown Sentient, while Slate's abilities focus on visions and knowledge.

"This Earth is developing drift science tech," continues Justice.

"My sentient already showed me that." In my head, images of cheering crowds appear from my sentient. They rarely beat out Slate in getting me news.

"Come on, now." Justice sighs. "You know what that means—most worlds destroy themselves once they reach this stage. Why save this planet?"

"Universes are born and die all the time," I counter. "Sentient pick which ones to save. Not us. You know that." While I chat with Justice, I can't help but notice how Axel keeps glaring at the office door. Something tells me I should take another look in there. "Unless you've got other news, I'm signing off."

"Hold your horses, now. Be reasonable. You're not like me and Slate."

My voice lowers. "I'm aware."

Both Justice and Slate are far stronger with sentient than I am. Hell, there are grandmas on my planet with more sentient power than I carry. And I get what Justice means. In this mission, he and Slate could escape an imploding planet much faster than I ever could. *Which is why I must succeed here or else.* I'm about to say precisely that when something happens.

The side office door opens. My sentient stop sending images of cheering crowds. Instead, fresh sensations course through me.

A buzz of excitement.

The pang of anticipation.

A rock-solid weight of willpower.

These aren't my emotions, though. It's all coming from my sentient. This is their way of saying, *the schism is close by.*

"Hold on," I tell Justice.

A girl steps through the newly-opened side door. She's the same teenager I counted before, only now I can catch a better look. She's young, red-haired, and wearing a poodle skirt. The name Emma is embroidered on her sweater. A pile of books and papers lie cradled in her arms. To my eyes, the documents glow with crimson light. As with Helen, my sentient are telling me that I found it.

The schism.

At last, this is familiar territory. If this mission is like Helen's, then those papers will carry drift science calculations. Once I fix a few numbers, then the schism will close. I check my watch once more.

Five minutes.

More than enough time.

Emma steps out the emergency back door. Axel stalks along after her, his thin tongue flickering hungrily over his heavy lips. I pause. On second thought, there may be more work here than simply fixing calculations. Axel and his buddies might put up a fight.

I take it back. That's a lot for five minutes.

Suddenly, long cracks form in the gym walls and ceiling. Red light peeps out through the fissures, casting odd patterns across the space. My pulse speeds. I've seen this effect before, and it means one thing.

This world is pulling apart.

On reflex, I scan the nearby faces. Everyone still goes about their business. Punching. Jumping. Lifting. The breaks are only visible to me, thanks to my sentient. Doesn't make them any less real, though.

"I got it," I tell Justice. "The schism centers on a girl named Emma; she just moved into an alley. Some guys trailed her. I'll go after them."

"No way." Justice's voice takes on a frantic note. "A bunch of guys sneak into a dark alley and you're following? You've no idea what kind of tech they're packing. I'm coming in to help you."

I prowl across the gym floor. More fissures appear beneath my feet. "Justice, I got this."

"No! Your hero complex is plum out of control. Give me your exact placelet location and—"

I click the earpiece off, ending our connection. As I march toward the back door, my brother's words echo through my mind.

Your hero complex is plum out of control.

Justice is wrong.

I don't have a hero complex.

It's more of a death wish.

My brothers and I make up the royal family of Umbra. We're expected to wield exceptional powers with sentient. Slate and Justice do; I don't. That makes me the chipped jewel in an otherwise-perfect crown.

I'm the extra prince.

Weak brother.

Unworthy royal.

Someone to be pitied as he's pushed aside.

Fuck that.

With each mission, I get one step closer to either proving myself a true royal ... or checking out of this game entirely. The question always hangs over me. Am I a real prince or a dead fool? Yanking on the back door, I step out into the darkened alley.

Maybe tonight's when things get settled, one way or another.

CHAPTER 2

"There are four kinds of sentient: black for battle, silver for knowledge, blue for visions, and red for schisms. Of these, most believe that red sentient are most powerful. They're wrong. Battle sentient, when wielded properly, make up the greatest force in the omniverse." – Wu Zhao Zetain, *The Art Of Sentient War*

STEPPING OUT THE DOOR, I enter the back alley. Blasts of hot air swirl around me. To my right, a narrow passage winds between two tall brick buildings. A sliver of night sky arches overhead. Humidity presses in, along with the scent of rotting garbage. Metal trash cans line one wall. Along the other, there's Axel and his gang. They surround Emma, who's gripping her books and papers against her chest like a shield.

Rage heats my veins. What kind of a guy corners a girl in an alley?

One who's about to get the crap beaten out of him, that's who.

I stalk closer. "Back off the girl."

Axel presses his meaty hands against the brick wall so his arms frame Emma's head. His gaze snaps in my direction. He growls out two words. "Keep walking."

Emma's shaking so badly, her papers rattle. She stares at me, her eyes wide with fear.

"You want me to leave, Emma?" I ask gently. She shakes her head. I refocus on Axel. "I'm staying."

"This bitch turned me down," grumbles Axel. "Called me an animal." He leans in until he's only inches away from Emma's face, then he boosts his voice to a shout. "No one gets away with that!" Emma gasps.

I stalk closer. "I said, back off the girl."

"No," snaps Axel. "You come closer, you'll get trouble."

Fresh cracks open along the walls. Thin beams of crimson light slice across the alley. No one else reacts to this change. They won't know what's happening until it's too late. My sentient start sending me a countdown. *This is it.* Only seconds remain to save this world.

Forty.

Closing my eyes, I summon my battle sentient. A moment later, particles rise up from my skin, forming a thin layer of black body armor. In the shadowy alley, no one can sense the change. But the battle sentient do more than protect my body. Energy pulses through my muscles. My mind focuses, dissecting attack vectors and defense plans. I tighten and release my fists, warming up. There are five of them. One of me.

I like these odds.

Two of Axel's lackeys rush in my direction. I knee the first guy in the gut, then pound my fist into the back of his skull. He falls over, unconscious. The second tries to catch me with an uppercut. I dodge the blow and give the guy a head-butt for his trouble. Number two tumbles over, completely out of it.

The cracks in the walls widen. Thin fissures open up into the night sky. My sentient send a new number into my mind.

Thirty.

The third lackey rushes at me. Fresh waves of power speed through my veins as I flip the guy over my shoulder, sending him skull-first against the asphalt. That guy's out cold, too.

The forth attacker is Ralph. The young kid's teeth are rattling, and not from cold.

"You want to run?" I ask.

He nods.

"So run."

Ralph passes me, pulls on the gym door, and takes off into the building.

Smart kid.

Overhead, huge swaths of red light cut across the night sky. A low rumble fills the air. My heart pulses so hard, I feel its beat in my throat. A new number appears from my sentient.

Twenty.

Axel sets his left hand against Emma's throat, locking her in place. With his right, he pulls out a gash razor. This is new tech. The blade not only slices, it burns through you with the force of a welding torch. This is off-world tech. And the letter K is emblazoned on the handle.

I step closer. "Where'd you get that?"

"None of your business." Axel swoops the blade toward my face; I dodge the blow.

Fresh images appear from my sentient. Axel recently found the gash dagger in the alley behind the gym. Chances are, Doc Zykin left it for him to find. The Komandir never do anything directly when they can use a patsy, and Doc Zykin really wants me dead.

Axel lunges for me, the razor gleaming in his fist. I duck out of the way. The blade passes a hair's breadth from my neck. Grabbing Axel's wrist, I twist his arm behind his back and press. The pressure makes him drop the gash razor. The weapon clangs onto the ground, useless. I slam my elbow against the back of Axel's skull. He slumps onto the gravel, unconscious.

Leaving Axel behind, I turn to Emma. "Are you all right?"

"Yes, thank you so much."

The threat should be over. It isn't though. Overhead, fresh breaks of crimson tear through the night sky. The rumble of thunder turns deafening. My sentient send me a new number.

Ten.

I frown. Axel is out cold. The schism should end. My thoughts race. *What am I missing?* Maybe I need to fix some calculations, like I did with Helen.

I refocus on Emma. "May I see your papers?"

She starts to hand them over but stops. "Watch out!" she cries.

Behind me, Axel hops back up to stand. This time, his appearance has changed. Once again, it's a difference only I can see. But what I witness? It's a nightmare that's come to life. Thin lines of red lightning wind about Axel's body, the strands fine as spider silk. The faint scent of charcoal fills the air. I've seen this before.

Something is trying to break through.

Or rather, someone.

Doc Zykin.

The Komandir faction wields special extra power over red sentient. Schism power. They love causing trouble. For years, they've tried to assassinate me. Goes with being the weak prince. I'm an easy target.

Damn. I was right all along. The Komandir are in on this.

The thin bolts of lightning merge across Axel's face, creating a new and familiar look. There's a hat with a rounded top and wide, flattened brim, along with a high collar suit. A long face then comes into focus: beady eyes and a grizzled chin that's accented with a moustache and goatee.

Doc Zykin is here, all right. My father's best friend and greatest enemy, all rolled into one.

The lightning version of Zykin grins. "Hickory dickory dock, the prince ran out the clock. Time ran out, the world went boom, hickory dickory dock."

This isn't as strange as it could be. Doc Zykin not only likes to plague my missions, he also speaks in nursery rhymes. I hate his fucking guts.

More of the web of lightning surrounds Axel. This is called bronya bonding. Komandir assassins use this technique to track someone down when there's no placelet data. Fortunately, I've seen this move before. Axel's body is like acting like a cosmic doorway. If I can close things down before they fully open, then Doc Zykin gets locked out of my reality.

I need to end this.

With all my focus, I pump all my battle sentient into my right arm. The muscles there twitch with held-in energy. Cocking my fist, I smack the mixture of Axel and Doc Zykin slap on the chin. The crack of bone breaking fills the air.

A moment later, the lightning bolts disappear from around Axel. He falls back onto the gravel, unconscious.

All around me, the red fissures close. Walls solidify. At last, the night sky becomes a single sheath of darkness—no breaks to be seen. My sentient send me an image of the open prairie behind my cabin back home: a rolling landscape covered in sheets of tall grass. It's one of my favorite views.

For my sentient, this is their way of saying, *it's over. We're safe.*

I let out a slow breath and turn to Emma. "Thanks for the warning."

"No, thank *you*." She offers me her papers. "Do you still want to see these?"

"Sure."

I take the sheets from Emma and give them a quick scan. Her numbers are flawless. She didn't need her calculations repaired, she only had to live long enough to share them. I flip through more pages.

"What will you do with these?" I ask.

"I got a scholarship to Zeta University," offers Emma. "It's part of a work study for Professor Hopkins. He's working on a machine that can open parallel universes."

I hold up the sheets. "Before Hopkins opens other worlds, make sure he sees these numbers. People often miss out on stabilizing dark matter and you nail it here. Stuff you do in the future can even ricochet the past, so be careful."

"Dark matter," Emma nods. "I'll remember."

A pair of figures step into the opposite side of the alley, their outline framed by moonlight. Emma waves in their direction. "My parents are here. I want to introduce them to you. Show them what happened. You're a hero, taking down those guys. Maybe you'll even get in the local news!" She rushes off to the other side of the alley.

Beep ... beep ... beep ...

As Emma rushes away, I tap my earpiece. "Accept comm."

"Get back here now," says Justice.

"What? No congratulations for saving another universe?"

"Cole is on his way."

That's my father and he has two modes. When we call him father, then he's acting like a regular dad. But when we call him Cole? That's an emperor who's having his consciousness eaten through by Crown Sentient. More and more, Cole only wants one thing. Blood.

"You need to close out your mission before he arrives," adds Justice.

"Understood." I click off the earpiece and pull on my sentient. A second later, a hoop of silver particles appears in the air before me. I'd worry about Emma seeing what I'm up to, but she's still chatting away with her parents on the other side of the alley.

Pulling on my sentient, I create the beginnings of a drift void, which is how we travel between universes. A circle of silver particles appears before me, which means the void's created by my knowledge sentient. I pump more energy into the connection. The particles spin in heavier loops until the center transforms into a solid panel of gray. The sight reminds me of a silver plate hanging in mid-air.

Then I punch through.

The silver panel smashes into tiny fragments, revealing a hole to another world. With our realities connected, I step between the round opening that now connects our realities.

Time to face Cole.

CHAPTER 3

"Managing the omniverse is only possible with a Visualization Dome. Through it, sentient graphically show us the most important paths and realities." – Hammurabi the Seventh, *Law of Sentient*

I STEP out the other side of the drift void and into the royal Viz Dome, a space that feels larger than a hover jet hangar. All around me threads of white light zoom and weave through the darkness. We call these reality bands, and they represent different timelines of parallel universes. The bands dart across the room in a great nest of interconnected worlds. Using this representation, the sentient show us which bands need attention in order protect the omniverse.

"Guys?" I call.

No reply from Justice or Slate.

My brothers aren't visible in the dome, but that's typical. When the Viz Dome is showing so many reality lines, it's like walking through a quickly-moving fog.

"There in a sec," drawls Justice at last.

"Minute," corrects Slate.

My younger brother isn't one for long sentences. One word is about what he gives at any time. And by saying *minute*, Slate means that he and Justice are examining other threads across the dome, and it will take them longer than a second to finish. In other words, Slate is a stickler for accuracy. I think it's a side effect of having control over vision sentient. The future is a disordered mess, so Slate keeps his present reality organized.

"Viz dome," I command. "Show planet X3894-B, strand BT704.35, and branch point 1T.783-50E."

A particular strand glows more brightly. I step closer, examining it with an expert eye. The thread looks stable. No pulse pattern or fading. The color's good, too. If Emma's world were still in trouble, the line would show red.

Thud ... Thud ... Thud ...

Someone's at the door.

One guess who.

The illusion of the nest of lines vanishes. In its place, my brothers and I now stand in a large gray space whose walls are made from shifting filaments. Nearby, Justice cuts a hefty figure in his long duster, heavy boots, and scarred face. Basically, he's a younger version of our father, Cole. Slate stands beside him. My younger brother is tall and sinewy with a long face and shoulder-length white hair. Like always, Slate wears a deep indigo jacket with a high collar and straight cut. Not for the first time, my brothers remind me of a cowboy and preacher from Umbra's old West days.

Or maybe we're based on an Earth version of the West. Hard to tell, what with so many lines of reality. Things get blurred.

Across the chamber, the wall threads pull apart. Cole steps through, his scarred face angry as thunder. Doc Zykin slinks along beside him. I'm happy to see that the Komandir assassin sports a nice bruise on his jawline. My punch back in Emma's world clearly connected.

Doc Zykin rubs his bony hands together. "Three blind mice, three blind mice. See how they hide, see how they hide. They all ran after their father's life, but he cut off their plans with a carving knife. Did you ever see such a sight in your life as three blind mice?"

This is Doc Zykin's way of accusing of trying to kill our father. The guy is a major prick.

"How's your chin, doc?" I ask. "Looks like a monster bruise."

Cole pauses a few yards away. Like Justice, the Emperor wears a long duster. Cole sets his hands on his hips, exposing the gash gun and bullets along his beltline. He rounds on me. "You got a problem with Doc Zykin?"

I nod. "He tried to kill me again."

If our world is based on the old West, then Doc Zykin is a classic snake oil salesman. It's not easy for father to handle the Crown Sentient. Eventually, every emperor goes mad. Supposedly, Doc Zykin gives father tonic that promote sanity. I doubt the doc's potions do anything, though. I think father just needs to believe there's a cure.

Cole's gaze flickers between me and the doctor. "I won't coddle you," says Cole at last. "You kill him or he'll kill you. That's how life works."

My heart sinks. No question about it. My father isn't here. This person before me is one hundred percent Cole. Months ago, my real dad would have told Zykin to back off. Not any more. We're losing our father my inches. What will disappear next?

"Enough whining." Cole scans me, Justice, and Slate in turn. "I tracked you three here for a reason."

"The emperor thinks you're plotting to take his throne," offers Doc Zykin.

Cole's eyes narrow to slits. "Not now, Doc."

Doc Zykin bows his head. "Yes, my Emperor." Only, the fake doctor moves slowly enough that I catch the smug grin on the old man's grizzled face. It's the Komandir faction who want the throne, not me and my brothers. Saying that never ends well, though.

"What do you need, Father?" asks Justice.

"My knowledge sentient say a request is coming," answers Cole. "I want y'all to ignore it."

"We serve the sentient," I say. "If they order us, we obey."

"This demand isn't from the sentient." Cole stares at the floor. It's what he does when he's about to lie his ass off. "I'm talking about a promise I made that's been fully kept. I don't owe anyone a thing. So none of you act on this, you hear me?"

My eyes widen. There's only one promise that Cole can mean here. It's how he got his Crown Sentient way from the Komandir in the first place. A pair of humans had developed enough drift science to contain Crown Sentient. As a favor to Cole, the humans stole the sentient and hid them in a lab. It worked. The Komandir never suspected the most powerful sentient in the omniverse were hiding in a backwater version of earth. But holding such power took a toll on Truman and Rose Archer. Their minds started to snap. The only way Truman could stay sane was to move to Umbra. His wife Rose is still back on Earth with their two daughters. My mother, Janais, checks on Truman. If a request for help is coming, it probably won't be from him.

"If Rose Archer asks for our help, then we must go to her aid," I say simply.

Cole's eyes turn wild. He lunges for me, his fists flying. I stand firmly in place. If Cole wants to hurt me, he will. It wouldn't be the first time.

Justice steps between us. "Let me talk to Thorne," he says to Cole. "Settle him down. No one will help Rose." Justice glares at me. "And if Thorne does try to aid Rose, then I'll put his sentient on lock down."

Lock-down is awful, by the way. You get an injection that deactivates your sentient. It's like having part of your soul torn away. No one's done it to me since I was a little kid, and then only because I couldn't control my powers. But seeing that fierce look in Justice's eyes? He'll do it now, no question.

Cole huffs out some rough breaths. "Lock down. That's good."

Doc Zykin wags his finger at me. "Baa baa, black sheep, have you any sense?"

Cole focuses on the Doc. "You got evening tonic?"

"Of course," replies Doc Zykin.

With that, the two step away toward the wall. As they get closer, the threads part, allowing them to leave. Within seconds, both Cole and Doc Zykin are gone.

For a long moment, I stare at the spot where they left. "I hate that guy."

"Which one?" asks Justice.

I tip my head. "Both, sadly." I focus on Slate. "Any new visions?"

"No," states Slate.

"Just the one still?" prompts Justice.

"Yes," confirms Slate.

We all know the vision Slate refers to. It has to do with Justice finding his transcendent. This is someone who's so important and beloved to you across so many parallel universes, the emotion between you bleeds into this reality. An Umbran transcendent will boost your powers, but even having a human one is a great gift. It's someone to share your thoughts, dreams and future. Slate's vision shows Justice finding his transcendent. If that happens, then my oldest brother could take over the Crown Sentient and give father some peace.

I can only hope that Slate's vision comes true.

CHAPTER 4

"The real purpose of royalty are to master and house vast numbers of sentient." –
Hammurabi the Seventh, *Law of Sentient*

BETWEEN THE ENCOUNTER with Cole and Doc Zykin—not to mention almost getting blown up by an imploding universe—I'm officially wiped out. I make my goodbyes to Slate and Justice, then I head back to my cabin. It's a solitary structure outside the official royal city of Fort Derringer. By the time I reach my front steps, it's well past midnight. Beyond log cabin, waves of tall grass sway in the moonlight. A full moon hangs low in the night sky.

My favorite view.

As I approach the door, the wooden slats transform into long brown filaments. The strands part as I approach, allowing me to enter. Like most things in Umbra, my cabin only appears old fashioned. On first glance, the interior is a simple square space made of rough-hewn logs. In reality, it's packed with more tech than a spaceship.

I step inside. "Rest, "I command.

The floorboards transform into filaments that rise up into the shape of a large bed, complete with comforter. All of a sudden, I can't believe how tired I am. I crawl under the covers and fall right asleep.

The next morning, I wake up fidgety and full of energy, so I make my way into Fort Derringer. The city is encircled by what looks like a tall wooden wall. Every so often, a crow's nest tower is set into the barrier, complete with a few guards. There's no formal gate, but there doesn't need to be one. The wall is made from filaments. As I approach, the strands detect my DNA signature. The strands part and allow me inside the compound proper.

Today, I'm back in my body armor again. Not that I expect trouble, but the people want to see that their weakest prince is always ready for a fight. Who am I to deny them?

Inside the fort, the streets are crowded with courtiers, meaning people in leathers or prairie gowns who want any number of things. Like trading contracts. More land. Fewer enemies. And always, they want more access to sentient power. Few make eye contact with me as I pass. I can almost see the thought bubbles above their heads.

Oh, that's just Thorne.

Not that I blame them. As a royal, the level of influence I wield is rather small.

I turn along the main dirt road, Oxblood Way. Up ahead there looms the Grand Palais. It looks like a music hall but it's really the official royal residence. I've had plenty of family time yesterday, so I skip the formal breakfast that's awaits me in the main dining hall. Instead, I grab an apple from a nearby cart and head over to a small round tent that reads, *Lord Wick's Amazing Strength Treatments*. Essentially, it's the Umbran version of Clyde's Gym.

The tent is a round affair with bright red stripes. Again, the filaments part as I approach. Stepping inside, I find a circular room that's ready for me to order it into whatever I require for exercise. The place is names for wicks, which are battle dummies. I quickly fall into my regular routine.

First, I command my sentient to reform into compression shorts. Easier for movement when practicing. After that, I order more battle sentient into the form of a long sword. Particles rise up from my skin, taking the shape of a samurai blade. Sentient can't form complex machines like rifles, but I always have a sword handy.

"Begin," I state.

The room responds. The brown threads of the floor come to life, rising up into the shape of a sparring partner. I bow to my faceless opponent. The sparring partner—my wick—does the same. I begin a series of warm-up lunges, followed by a speed round of thrusts and parries. My wick keeps pace.

The wall to my right shimmies. The threads there divide, pulling apart as a new person enters the space. It's my mother, Janais.

She looks regal at all times, what with her strong cheekbones, copper skin, and long neck. Today Mother wears a brown robe with lace at her throat. The garment's train twists as it follows behind her.

For a few seconds, Mother watches me practice. Then she speaks. "Your reaction times are getting better," she says in her deep alto.

I keep on practicing. "Why are you here?" Mother doesn't stop by without a reason.

"You must convince Justice. Your older brother listens to you."

This is an old conversation, and I'm simply not in the mood. "Convince him to kill father? No one can do that." I make another lunge at the wick and miss. Big mistake. The sparring dummy gets a strike in on my left shoulder. That's the first serious hit the wick has gotten in. *Damn. This conversation is shattering my focus.*

As it should.

Who wants to kill their own father?

Mother presses on. "That's why the three of you must do it together. You, Justice, and Slate. Be secretive and surprise him." She lifts her chin, but there's no missing the wobble in her voice. "Your father is suffering. This is the only way to give him peace."

Mother is resigned that saving Cole is hopeless, yet I can't accept that. *I won't.* On reflex, I shift into an aggressive set of strikes. The wick steps backward. "Father may be saved yet. Slate thinks there's hope."

"Your baby brother is a dreamer."

"His visions often come true."

"Only when he has them time and again. But Slate only had one vision—just one—where there was a transcendent mate. A brief flash of a single reality where Justice found his transcendent, a mystery woman to match Justice's power, making my eldest son strong enough to defeat Cole without killing him. That's a false dream. Transcendents don't exist."

Rage spikes through my limbs. I strike a killing blow through the wick's chest. The sparring dummy melts back into the floor. I turn to my mother, pulling in deep breaths from exertion. "But what if Slate's vision is true? Justice could have someone who balances him out. Someone who does—"

"What I thought I could do for your father?" Mother shakes her head. "I wanted to be his transcendent. I wasn't. There's no such thing, my son."

"My brothers and I are all in agreement. We'll help patrol the omniverse, keeping the worlds safe. That will buy us time to find a transcendent for Justice."

"That won't work," counters Mother. "Cole already fears Justice will assassinate him. He keeps attacking your brother. Soon one of them will perish. You will choose which." She steps closer. "You fight well in a simulation, my son. No one works harder at their studies. But that is all you can do. There are palace servants with more power over the sentient. The only way your life has purpose is if you convince your brothers to act when the time comes. You must save Justice. He's the eldest. It's his destiny to be Emperor."

I meet Mother's gaze straight on. For this next statement, she needs to know that I mean what I say. "I would never stand by while Justice died."

My meaning is simple. If it comes to Justice or Cole, there's no question where my loyalties will fall. Justice.

Mother exhales. "Don't wait too long, then. And please don't place your hopes in those silly visions from Slate." She snaps her fingers; a section of wall opens up once again. Mother starts to leave; then she pauses once more. "I was harsh before. I know you work hard to compensate for your lack of power. If only you weren't so weak with sentient, you could have been the greatest Emperor of them all."

With that, Mother steps away. I'd say her words stung, but I've heard them before. The pain is part of a dull ache that I carry with me always.

In the very spot on the wall where Mother departed, a silver loop of particles appears. A drift void. I frown. No one should be able to open one of those inside the royal compound. The loop widens until someone appears on the other side of the void.

I gasp.

I'd know that face anywhere.

It's Rose Archer.

CHAPTER 5

"A debt is a sacred bond. One must always repay what is owed." – Emperor Cole, first official address to the people of Umbra

YET IS that really Rose Archer?

Perhaps this is a trick of the mind.

I blink.

Take a deep breath.

Refocus.

But Rose Archer is still there, visible through the center of the swirling drift void. It's like some bizarre version of an enchanted mirror from a fairy tale. Only instead of seeing an evil queen or lost princess, I'm looking at none other than Rose Archer, one half of the scientist team who won my father his throne.

My knowledge sentient have shown her to me before. Sometimes when I meet with my father—and he's acting like my father, not Cole—Dad will talk about his decision to become Emperor. The Komandir Emperor, Valerik VII, had gone on a killing spree, destroying all universes with intelligent life. So father came up with the idea to siphon off the Crown Sentient into a hiding place. He visited a version of Earth where only two souls understood drift science, Rose and Truman Archer. Father convinced them to help.

At this point in Father's story, my vision sentient would send me images of Rose and Truman. She's lean and elegant with long brown hair and intelligent ebony eyes. Truman has blond hair, broad shoulders, and always wears small round glasses. Mother visits him every so often, and my sentient give me updated images of his face. Truman's hair is now white and he stoops, but that scientific mind is still clear in his intelligent gaze.

A different Rose stares at me through the drift void. She's a hollow copy of the one who helped Father. Her calm elegance is replaced with manic focus, like a human spring that's coiled too tightly. Her frantic look makes me wonder. Are others getting this vision from Rose as well? Mostly, I worry about Father and Doc Zykin. The Komandir love to pounce on weakness, and Rose isn't looking her best. If others can see this message, there will be trouble and fast.

One way to find out.

Reaching forward, I touch the void. The swirling silver particles feel cool against my skin. My sentient should show me images of others who see this same message. There's nothing, though; only me. Rose drops a strand of hair into the connection between us. Another image pops into my mind. It's Rose's daughter Luci, who is the spitting image of her father, Truman. The loop of sentient change from silver to red.

Whatever has happened to Luci, she's in trouble.

The drift void flares more brightly. After that, it vanishes. The message is over. Rose Archer is gone. Leaning back on my heels, I stare at the conical ceiling and think through my options. The way I see it, there are two ways this could go.

First, I could report this as an official mission and add it to the Viz Dome tracking system. That's the correct protocol for this situation. My family would then know about Rose's request, as would anyone with access to the Viz Dome, including Doc Zykin. If I did that, there's no question what would happen next, though. Or to be accurate, what would *not* happen.

No one would help Rose.

If anything, she'd end up dead.

Not on my watch.

Which leaves me with option two: open a drift void and sneak off to Rose's world in my own. I can leave a fake mission in the Viz Dome. This way, I'll be able to keep Father's promise and do the right thing. And since I know how to hide my placelet data, I won't be found unless I wish it.

With that thought, it's settled.

I'm visiting Rose's version of Earth. If there's one thing I've learned about my powers, it's that actions have a ripple effect across the past and future. Good actions cause positive things; evil brings on more pain and death. It's one thing to know this intellectually; it's another to spend your life inside a Viz Dome where you see a singular evil ripple through billions of lives.

Rose and Truman made a massive sacrifice for my family.

It's a debt that must be paid.

Reaching forward, I summon my sentient and issue a silent command.

Open a drift void. Take me to Rose Archer.

CHAPTER 6

"A mission may seem routine. Yet one should always expect the unexpected." –
Beauregard the Great, *Instructions for Visiting Parallel Worlds*

THIS TIME, I whisper the words aloud. "Take me to Rose Archer."

A loop of silver sentient appears before me. Millions of tiny particles swirl about in a two-dimensional whirlpool. Soon more sentient join the movement until a tall round plate floats the air before me. I'm in no rush, so I don't *have* to punch my way through.

But it's enjoyable.

I slam my fist against the reflected surface. The plate shatters into thousands of tiny fragments, revealing a different world on the other side of the void, namely a dreary and empty kitchen. After ordering my battle sentient to form body armor, I step through the portal between our two universes. My boots thud onto the tiled floor of Rose's Earth.

The portal closes behind me, sealing me off in this reality.

Stepping about in a slow circle, I scan my new surroundings. This kitchen is a small space. There are a few sticks of mismatched furniture, including a tall chair perched by a greasy window. Against the walls, someone has shoved appliances that have seen better days. I frown. Rose and Truman were well-to-do when they helped father. What happened to them?

Fortunately for me, there's one easy way to find out.

Knowledge sentient make excellent snoops.

Lifting up my arm, I set my palm parallel to the floor. After that, I command my knowledge sentient to fall. Tiny silver particles cascade from my fingertips to reach the ground. After that, the sentient start to dig. Within seconds, they've found themselves a main data line deep underground. Once they jack into the info feed, facts about this world pour into my head. It's an art form to separate useless and critical info, but I quickly get a solid read on this planet.

Turns out, I'm on a version of Earth that's about as far away from the prime reality as you can get. That's no shock, by the way. In fact, it's why Father chose this world in the first place. Back when Rose and Truman helped Father, this continent was called the United Americas. Now a new government runs the place, the Authority. They strive for purity in all things and purge anyone who doesn't meet their standards. Rose would be considered mentally unbalanced, so she definitely should have been killed by now.

So how is Rose alive and safe?

I scan more records, looking for answers. Turns out, the building I stand in was once a chemical manufacturing plant. Now, it's an abandoned ruin. The plant is also off grid, meaning it's outside the government's search range. So someone is keeping Rose safe by hiding her out here. Was that Luci?

The kitchen door rattles. *Someone's here.* I command my knowledge sentient to return to my body. In a flash of silver, the tiny particles rise up from the floor and rejoin my hand. I don't have enough sentient that I can sacrifice them easily, especially if this intruder is unfriendly.

The door swings open; an elderly woman steps inside. She's stooped and underfed with short gray hair and a loose housecoat.

Definitely not someone I need to worry about fighting.

She gasps when she sees me; then recovers herself. "Pardon me," she says. "I'm Miss Edith. You must be one of Luci's gentleman callers."

Luci. That's the name Rose sent through the drift vortex. "Where is Luci?"

"Ran off months ago." The way Miss Edith says those words, it's clear she doesn't approve of Luci's actions.

I tilt my head, thinking this through. Based on Miss Edith's revelation, I've been called here to find a missing person. That shouldn't be too hard. My knowledge sentient hacked into the planet's information systems rather quickly. More in depth searches should be possible, assuming that I can find our build the right equipment. It's something I've faced on many previous missions.

Yes, finding Luci will be more than possible.

Looking up, I realize that Miss Edith has been staring at me for some time. She still expects an answer to her question.

"I'm *not* one of Luci's gentleman callers," I explain.

Miss Edith pulls out a dented teapot and fills it in the utility sink. She raises a chipped teacup toward me. Miss Edith doesn't speak, but I get what she's asking. *Do you want any tea?*

I nod.

A voice echoes in from the factory floor. "No tea for me this morning, Miss Edith." The speaker is a young girl. At the sound of her voice, my sentient kick into action, sending me an overwhelming array of images. There's a sign for the Learning Squirrel High School, a hefty man in overalls, and the sight of the Ozymandias Chemical Plant as it fluctuates in and out of existence. This building has been flipping into two-dimensional space time. Why?

"It's not for you," calls Miss Edith.

"Mom doesn't want any either," adds the girl.

If my sentient were active before, now they go positively berserk. The images come too quickly for me to process. Leaning against a nearby counter, I close my eyes tightly, trying to focus.

"The tea is for your guest," explains Miss Edith.

Someone taps at my elbow. Forcing the barrage of images aside, I open my eyes to see Miss Edith standing beside me with a tea cup in her hand. I take the drink from her. "Thank you."

Looking up, I focus on the pair of figures that now stand in the kitchen doorway.

And my world turns upside down.

CHAPTER 7

"Simply put, finding one's transcendent is the greatest gift the omniverse can ever bestow." – Empress Ophelia, *The Lost Book Of Transcendence*

ROSE ARCHER LEANS against a teenage girl with brown hair, ebony eyes, and lovely curves. My sentient, which had been losing it before, now fall silent. Blue sentient rise up from my skin. I don't ask them to do this; they make the movement on their own.

Sentient acting without commands? That simply doesn't happen.

My sentient float across the room to hover around the girl. Our gazes lock. Parts of my soul twist. Energies shift. Connections form. My sentient whirl about her, creating a thin haze around her body. The sight sends a pang of shock up my torso. This isn't supposed to happen. Once sentient bond to their host, they aren't able to move without a command. Yet mine did.

New emotions whirl through me. They aren't mine. With a sense of rightness, I realize the truth. These feelings come from the girl.

I feel the numbness of exhaustion.

Perk of interest.

And a chill of fear.

I can only stare at this girl in awe. My sentient move and I feel her emotions? That can't be right. Something on this planet must be messing with my head.

Sharing sentient and emotions only happens with your transcendent.

And of all Umbrans, I'm the last person to find their perfect match.

Even so, the girl's emotions keep whirling through my nervous system. Meanwhile, experiences appear in my mind. Only trouble is, they aren't mine, either. This is nothing like the scenes my sentient sent before. What I receive is more of a pre-packaged memory, only one that's never happened. In my mind's eye, I see a burst of light as the first experience slams into my soul.

Flash. It's nighttime. The girl and I ride hoverbikes side by side high over a strange city. Lights blink beneath us. We're laughing.

Flash. The girl and I stand on a sandy landscape. Both of us hold swords. We're back-to-back and ready for battle.

Flash. It's an empty dance floor. An orchestra plays a slow tune. I wear a tuxedo; she's in a black dress. We dance slowly, our arms wound around each other, her head resting on my shoulder.

My skin prickles over with awe. This must be transcendence. I've lived so many other realities with this girl, our emotions and experiences are bleeding over to this world. I scan her again, more carefully this time. Even in baggy human jeans and a threadbare shirt, she's the most beautiful woman I've ever seen. And the best part? This experience is definitely a first for her as well, yet she doesn't cower in terror. Instead she stares at me, fearless and wary.

No wonder I love this girl across so many universes.

She's a wonder.

With this girl, the best parts of both our souls can become amplified. Hell, they already have in other realities. Now it just needs to happen here. Everything in me wants to crumple onto my knees and thank whatever rules the omniverse for this mighty gift. But the girl still wears a worried look. Clearly, she has no idea what's happening. Also, this girl called Rose 'her mother' before. That means my transcendent is a human.

Not that I care.

Sharing my soul is enough of a boon. This girl can have my sentient as well, although I have precious little to share with her. The fact that she doesn't have any sentient to give back to me? That doesn't matter in the slightest. I'll have her.

I'll have *us*.

The girl shakes her head, breaking our connection. The blue sentient pull back into my body. My brows lift. This girl just commanded my sentient. Normally, it takes an Umbran years of practice to learn how to manipulate their own sentient, let alone someone else's.

The girl walks her mother over to a chair by the window. After sitting down, Rose focuses on me for the first time. "Thank you so much for coming," she says. "You look just like Cole."

"He's my father." I bow slightly in her direction. "Thorne Oxblood, at your service."

Miss Edith takes another sip from her tea sup. "I like this one," she says to the girl. "You can ignore that MacGregor boy."

I arch my brows. "MacGregor?"

"It's nothing," the girl says quickly. "Thanks for the tip, Miss Edith." A blush colors her cheeks. It's beyond lovely.

Rose presses her forehead against the windowpane by her chair. When she next speaks, she doesn't look in my direction. "Can you help us?"

What focus. Having touched Crown Sentient, every cell in Rose's body must be craving a visit to Umbra. I'd imagine it's a chorus that drowns out all other thoughts. How impressive for her to stay this coherent.

"I can make good on your pact with my father," I reply. The ghost of a smile rounds Rose's mouth. She cares for her daughter's safety. Which confirms my theory as to why Rose stayed here for so long—she wants to protect her children.

Which reminds me.

My transcendent.

Little by little, I turn to face the girl. Part of me is certain she'll have disappeared in the few seconds I spoke to Rose. After all, I don't deserve a transcendent. Having her vanish would be expected.

Yet she's still here.

Our gazes meet again. *This girl is real.* I swallow past the knot of amazement in my throat. When I next speak, I take care to gentle my voice. "And you are?"

The girl's blush deepens. I want to kiss the pink hue along her neck. My sweet transcendent.

"She's Meimi Archer," explains Miss Edith.

The moment freezes. My transcendent is Meimi Archer. I turn the name around in my mind. It's lovely and strong, just like my transcendent.

"Rose here is her mother," continues Miss Edith. "I'm the hired help. More tea?"

Her words remind me that I haven't touched the first round I'd taken. I set the cup onto the counter behind me. "No, thank you," I reply.

"Such a sweet boy." Miss Edith turns to Meimi. "But you should watch those security systems of yours. He walked right into this building."

In truth, I created a drift void to enter the building. Still, the question of security is an important one. My sentient grow restless at the thought of Meimi unprotected.

For her part, Meimi steps closer to Miss Edith. "You didn't notice anything about the building when you came in?"

That raises yet another question. What's bothering my transcendent? Before, I'd detected a chill of fear from Meimi. I'd also seen a vision from my sentient of this building flipping into two-dimensional space-time. Perhaps that's what has Meimi so concerned. Most likely, the Authority doesn't approve of rogue scientists working off-grid.

"No, should I have?" asks Miss Edith.

Meimi shrugs. "Just making conversation. And you're right—I'll look into the security systems. In the meantime, can you please get Mom a blanket?"

Miss Edith takes another sip from her teacup. "She doesn't look cold."

"Mom and I need a moment alone with Thorne."

My brows lift. *This ought to be interesting.*

"Ah, I understand." Miss Edith wags her finger at Meimi. "No funny business while I'm gone."

"Meaning?" asks Meimi.

Miss Edith lifts her chin. "No kissing."

I fight the urge to smile, but not too hard. Miss Edith is rapidly becoming a favorite.

Meimi's blush deepens even further. *So lovely.* "Thank you, Miss Edith. I'll remember that."

Miss Edith shuffles from the room, humming as she goes. I get the distinct impression that this is a rather exciting morning for her. Once Miss Edith is well and truly gone, Meimi turns to me once more. "Mom called you here to find my sister Luci."

I nod. "She's the DNA sample you sent."

"Can you find lost humans ... I mean missing, uh, people ... Earthlings?" She twists her fingers at her waistline while speaking. It's adorable.

"I can do all sorts of things. Let me demonstrate." Closing my eyes, I order my sentient to take a new form. My black body armor shimmers, then it takes the form of dark jeans, a black Henley, and heavy boots. I gesture across my torso. "I have synthetic and organic micromachines that are merged with my nervous system. We call them the sentient. With their help, I can create armor, tap into computer systems, and even break through some kinds of walls. I will find your sister."

Meimi nibbles at her lower lip, thinking this through. My instinct is to cup her face in my hands, but I fight away the urge. This is already a lot for anyone to process. A full minute passes before I speak again.

"I'll start looking for your sister once I set up some additional systems."

"Do you need any equipment?" asks Meimi. "My lab is downstairs and I have some gear there."

"Thank you," I state. "That would be very helpful. While I'm at it, Miss Edith brought up a good point. I suggest some security enhancements to the factory. I can link in some of my sentient to the system and track intruders more efficiently." I stare at my feet. "I don't have many sentient, but the ones I have are effective."

"I'm sure they're amazing." Meimi gives me a half-smile and I want to shout with joy. "Any security upgrades you can make would be great."

Miss Edith blusters back into the room, bringing Rose a blanket. She then shoots me and Meimi a knowing stare. "You two look cozy." Miss Edith then mouths the words: *keep saving yourself for this one.*

My brows lift. Did Miss Edith just announce that Meimi's a virgin?

Meimi's eyes widen. All the color drains from her face.

Yes, that's exactly what Miss Edith did. This lady cracks me up. Even so, I press my lips together, biting back my smile.

Meimi starts toward the door. "Oh, wow. Just got a message from my smart watch."

Miss Edith sips her tea and grins. "I didn't hear any beeps. Doesn't your watch ding when you get an alert?"

Meimi's mouth falls open, a movement that means *yes, her watch does ding when she gets an alert.* Meimi then hugs her elbows and sighs. It's a movement that means one thing. *I keep messing up.*

That said, I wish Meimi wouldn't be so hard on herself. With all that's happened today, I think Meimi's handling it all extremely well. I have hardened warriors who would have collapsed the moment our consciousness merged.

"I'll just take off for school now," says Meimi.

Alarm bells ring through my nervous system. My transcendent is not roaming around this world without protection. "You're going to school alone?" I ask. "Where are your guards?" Justice and Slate have at least two bodyguards at any point in time. I refuse mine, but that's beside the point. Meimi is my transcendent. She should be protected.

"Guards?" Meimi shrugs. "This is a Learning Squirrel High School. The only thing you need to guard me from is our science teacher, the Bummer." She makes little quotation marks with her fingers when she says, *the Bummer.*

If this is supposed to stop me from worrying, it doesn't.

"Guards," I repeat.

Scooping up her backpack from the floor, Meimi opens the sack and shows me the interior. "Weapons," she states.

I step closer and take a look. An array of chem darts, smoke bombs and gash guns are packed into the bag's interior. It makes the razor that Axel was wielding look like a plastic knife.

Miss Edith totters over to stand beside us. "Are those chem darts? Can I play with them?"

"Sure you can," Meimi says. "But later." She refocuses on me. "Are we good?"

I scan the contents of the backpack once more. Many of these devices look hand made, probably by Meimi herself. Clearly, my transcendent is a force to be reckoned with. An in truth, Meimi can probably handle one more day at her miserable high school. Meanwhile, I can use the time get my systems set up.

Meimi refocuses on me. "Are we good?"

"For now." Once I get more information, things will change around here. There's no way my transcendent is meandering around this world alone.

"See you," Meimi calls. Hoisting up her backpack, she speeds for the door. It's the same one Miss Edith used to enter the kitchen this morning. I hadn't felt anything when Miss Edith entered. But watching Meimi leave? It sets my nerves on edge.

I can't shake the feeling that Meimi isn't going to Learning Squirrel High School at all. There's still something else that's worrying her. Most likely, it has to do with contacting me and flipping the building into two-dimensional space-time.

Only one way to find out for certain.

Get more information.

CHAPTER 8

"Never rely on sentient alone for success. You must also master technology, history and—most of all—psychology." – Beauregard the Great, *Instructions for Visiting Parallel Worlds*

I WATCH Meimi leave through the small window set into the kitchen door. She walks off into the labyrinth of old brick buildings surrounding the main chemical plant. I still hate to see her depart. It's wrong somehow.

Miss Edith steps up behind me. "Want directions to Meimi's lab?"

I turn around. "Very much."

She purses her wrinkled lips. "Do you want some breakfast first?"

"No, thank you." My sentient can keep me fed for days at a time, not that I'll explain that to Miss Edith. "Just directions."

"Head across the factory floor. The far-right corner to the building. Emergency exit. Take the stairs to the furnace room."

I narrow my eyes. "Furnace room?"

"The place is completely safe. Our Meimi is a genius, you know."

I lift my chin. "Of course, she is." Miss Edith grins so hard, I'm surprised her face doesn't crack. I give myself a mental slap. I can't make it too obvious that Meimi is my transcendent. Not that I worry what Miss Edith will do, but it's everyone else in the omniverse I have to worry about.

Especially my father and Doc Zykin.

Worry tightens up my spine. If either Cole or the Komandir faction discovers that I have a transcendent, then Meimi will be marked for death and quickly. It doesn't matter that Meimi is human. The fact that I have a transcendent will be the same as announcing that I wish to take father's place as Emperor. All the more reason to get to work on finding more data to protect her.

"If you'll excuse me," I say.

"Sure thing." Miss Edith is still grinning far too widely.

As I take off into the main factory floor, Miss Edith calls after me. "If you need any equipment or parts, then I have contact numbers for Chloe and Zoe."

Pausing, I turn to face Miss Edith again. "Chloe and Zoe?"

"Meimi's best friends. They're also geniuses. And single." She keeps smiling, and there's something sneaky in her grin. "In case you have any brothers."

I shake my head. *Miss Edith is too much.* "Note taken."

Miss Edith steps back into the kitchen, and I resume my march across the factory floor. The place is all huge vats and rusted pipes. I pick my way through the maze until I find the emergency exit door. After stepping inside, I follow the staircase down to the basement level. Essentially, Meimi's workroom is a rusted concrete box filled with broken-up parts. Monolith towers lay open, their wire innards spilling out. Gears sit in a pile in one corner, chip boards are stacked in another. The walls are lined with hooks that suspend all sorts of tools.

I inspect the monolith towers first, but my sentient are having none of it. They keep sending me images of men in trench coats approaching the doors. It's clear they have their own priorities.

Fixing the security system.

Now, my plan was to get some monoliths working so I could get more information on Meimi and this factory. In particular, I want to know why Meimi is so concerned that the place flipped into two-dimensional space-time. That said, my sentient are rarely this intrusive.

Best to give them what they want.

I pick through the piles on the floors, finding enough bits to create hand and retinal scanners. I even add in some of my own knowledge sentient into the system. It's hard to separate even a particle from my body, but it is the best way to keep the place secure. My sentient can also act as video monitors anywhere there's access wire, which is essentially all around the building.

With the security in place, I focus the monoliths. *What a mess.* All the good parts seem to have been recently scoured from the main systems. Looking at the papers around, I'm guessing Meimi is a scientist for hire. Most likely, she'd had to raid these monoliths for parts many times over. Which means I'm on a hunt for usable tech. Stepping around, I rescan the piles of supplies lining the room. It takes a while, but I find enough to start work on one monolith. I've just begun when my knowledge sentient send me images of Meimi approaching the building.

Now, much as I'd love to pause here and greet Meimi properly, I'd rather have a functioning monolith that helps keep her safe. So I keep attaching a data replicator to the dark matter spine inside the monolith I'm working on. This is tricky stuff. A few minutes later, Meimi pushes open the heavy metal door to this chamber. I'm almost finished with the data replicator, so I stay head-first inside the monolith.

"How's it going?" Meimi asks.

"Slowly," I explain. "Your systems need a ton of upgrades. There's not much I can do without the right gear."

Meimi takes in a deep breath. "Look, maybe I should have said this before, but I was a little distracted. You should know that Mom and I flipped this factory into two-dimensional space-time. Now our government may be sending over soldiers to pick up everyone. Although I hope they don't because I just made a deal with a criminal overlord named the Scythe to prevent that."

I drop the replicator.

Soldiers may be picking up Meimi and her family?

Getting protection from a criminal overlord?

What the ever-loving hell?

Leaning out of the monolith, I look up at Meimi. Once again, my vision sentient connect us. My emotions siphon off from my nervous system.

There's the fire of protective rage.

Electric jolts of affection.

The chill of determination.

Meimi takes a half-step backward. "These feelings..." she stammers. "What do they mean?"

When I next speak, I place all my heart into the words. "That I don't care who's coming or what the risks are. I won't leave you, Meimi."

Meimi gasps and the transcendent connection between us vanishes. Clearly, she's still frightened. My poor Meimi.

I rise. "You're mine to protect."

"Why would you say that? You don't know me."

I lock my gaze with hers. "The past, present, and future are all constructs. In some dimensions, they all exist at the same moment."

Meimi nods. "Sure, that's one of the first things you learn in drift science."

"In many of these other places and dimensions, you and I already know each other. In fact, our connection is so strong, it's bleeding over into this reality. My people call it *finding your transcendent*. It's incredibly rare. Not to mention, unexpected." I give her a sad smile. "Especially for me."

Meimi sets her hands on her throat. "Something happened between us in the kitchen, too. Was that true, or am I having some kind of hallucination?"

"It's true." I step closer. "It happened."

"This isn't the first time either," continues Meimi. "The Authority— that's our government—has this genetically enhanced attack animal called the Lacerator. Not an animal exactly; it's more like a particle monster." She huffs out a breath. "This is so hard to explain."

"Did it look like this?" On my arm, I make my Henley change back into body armor. "Now, I'll slow the process down." Once the transformation moves more slowly, Meimi can clearly see the tiny particles that hover over his skin as they realign into a new shape.

"Definitely. That's what the Lacerator looked like."

"That wasn't a monster. It's what I was telling you about before. The sentient. Most exist in a swarm. Most likely, this Lacerator of yours is an independent cyber swarm." I move even nearer. "If they're interested, a swarm can choose to link to people for short periods of time."

Meimi blinks hard. Clearly, she's trying to process this news. "So all that was real."

"This is a lot of information," I say gently. "We can discuss it another time. I don't wish to overwhelm you."

"No, I can do this." She lifts her chin and meets my gaze. Her brown eyes flash with fire. She's brilliant.

"Tell me," I say gently. "What happened when you encountered the Lacerator?"

"I could feel its emotions. Images also appeared in my mind. It was some way of communicating with me. But with you, it was different. I got these crazy visions of us doing things together."

I shake my head. "You must have so many questions."

"I do, but I'm also in trouble. If you can find Luci and manipulate the sentient, maybe you can help with this." She zips open her backpack, pulls out a data pad, and hands it to me. "I told you I made a deal before. Here's what it is. If I can build this by midnight, then the Merciless won't attack my home. Can you help me?"

When I accessed the city systems, I saw images of the Merciless. They're heartless killers disguised as police. "So you don't wish to run away?" I ask.

"No, I'm staying here. The Scythe will find me wherever I go, and besides, this is my home."

I picture all the equipment in Meimi's pack, plus the things I found in here. "I could counter attack."

"Not the Authority and not within a matter of hours." Meimi firms up her stance. "This is my plan. Will you help?"

I meet her gaze once more. "Yes, I will."

I'd do anything for you.

"Excellent." Meimi's shoulders slump with relief.

And so, we begin working together.

CHAPTER 9

"Transcendence is the natural unification of two seemingly unrelated souls." –
Empress Ophelia, *The Lost Book Of Transcendence*

WE JUMP RIGHT into building the prototype. Meimi sorts through piles
of parts around the room. I keep reviewing the schematic on her data
pad. According to the readout, we're supposed to finish this thing in a
matter of hours. Based on what I saw before, we don't necessarily have
enough raw materials here. Meimi picks at another knot of wires, pauses
and sighs.

I step up to her side. "Do you wish to also contact Chloe and Zoe? I
understand they have skills that may be useful."

Meimi's eyes widen. "Who told you about them?" She then holds out
her arm, palm forward, in a motion that means *hold on*. "Let me guess.
Miss Edith told you?"

I bite back a chuckle. "Before you arrived, Miss Edith was, uh, very
forthcoming with information."

"Ugh, I don't want to know. Let's get to work."

"Let's." I beam with delight. *Amazing. I'm actually working on a project
with my transcendent.* It's more than I ever imagined for my life, let alone
this trip to Earth. Meimi meets my gaze. Lines of pure joy wind between
us. My transcendent blushes. It's rapidly becoming my favorite look
on her.

"I have some diagrams on my worktable." She says at last. "We can
adapt them."

"Sounds like a plan."

Back home, I do a lot of tinkering myself. For basic stuff like the monolith, silence is fine. However, what we're about to build is rather complex. For tricky projects, music is a requirement. Before, I'd noticed a kind of ancient player hanging from a wall hook. I step up and gesture toward it.

"Music?" I ask.

Meimi nods. "I need a beat when I work."

Pursing my lips, I hit the *Play* button. It's ancient Earth stuff with a heavy beat, something called *Seven Nation Army*.

Meimi winces. "Too loud?"

I smile. "No, it's perfect."

Back in Umbra, I often work with my brothers. It rarely goes well. Justice tries to run things. Slate slinks off to a corner and does what he likes. I end up running between them, trying to coordinate the chaos of three strong personalities across one objective. However, it's not that way with Meimi and me. Our work is more of an intricate dance than anything else. I take apart an exotic matter detector; Meimi writes code for a power burst.

We don't talk.

Music thrums through us.

We get things done.

Every once in a while, our hands or bodies brush, and it sends an electric charge of excitement through me. Watching Meimi work is simply dazzling. She takes three unrelated items, modifies them quickly, and creates something even I've never seen before. And I've seen quite a lot. Her results are rough, but they're always both effective and revolutionary. Meanwhile, my creations are fast, orderly and functional.

All in all, we make a pretty good team.

Every so often, my thoughts fly back to my original purpose for this trip. I'm supposed to find Luci. Once I get that monolith working, I will do just that. But will Meimi want to join me on the search for her sister? There are so many things I want to know about my transcendent, and teaming up to find Luci would give me a chance to ask some of the many questions buzzing around my head.

What does Meimi like to read?

How has she avoided the Authority for so long?

When did she meet Chloe and Zoe?

I picture us on my hoverbike, tooling around the countryside of New Massachusetts while locating Luci. It's a tempting image, but it's one that must wait. The prototype needs to come first.

The hours stream by, and before I know it, Meimi is installing a big red button atop the sealed briefcase. Turns out, she's a big believer of making it easy to know how her inventions get activated. Love it.

Inside the briefcase, the device is a careful weave of circuit boards and wires. Meimi and I ran a ton of diagnostic tests. No question about it. This thing will create a massive drift void at midnight on Saturday night at the Learning Squirrel High School.

When midnight comes around, my new security system talks through a freshly installed comm unit on the wall.

"Meimi, someone's approaching the back entrance."

The smooth voice startles Meimi out of writing instructions for her underworld contact. She sets the pages aside, punches off the music and turns to me. "I got this. It's Fritz."

Meimi mentioned him a few times. He's the heavy for the Scythe, Meimi's illegal employer. I hate the idea of her interacting with these folks, but it's too late now. The only thing I can do at this point is ensure she'll be safe.

"I won't be far away," I promise.

Meimi closes up the briefcase and speeds away. I follow at a careful distance, making sure to stick to the shadows. Underworld types are notoriously skittish. I don't want this Fritz getting jumpy. As we near the back entrance, the rumble of rain sounds on the metal roof. Meimi opens the door to reveal a blocky man with a shock of white hair and jean overalls. Fritz.

"You got it, ya?" His accent is obviously a false one.

"Yes, instructions are here." Meimi hands him a padded envelope and then turns over the briefcase. "I still hate the idea of Godwin having this."

Meimi explained about this before. Godwin is the ultimate buyer for this item. He also works for the Authority. Normally, I'd send more sentient out to get information on Godwin, but all my focus was needed for the prototype.

"Don't worry," says Fritz. "He won't use it. Just wants to run diagnostics." From my hiding spot in the shadows, I can see guilt flash in Fritz's beady eyes.

Not good.

Meimi shifts her weight from foot to foot. "Actually, that makes me *more* nervous than before. The Scythe said the Authority would actually use the thing. What's this really about?"

"Proof of your skills, Meimi." Fritz speaks far too quickly to be believable, though. Something else is at work here. "Don't worry, we'll all get rich off this."

Fritz shoves the briefcase and envelope under his coat and then turns away. Meimi watch him trudge off into the rain-soaked night. I step out of the shadows and pause just behind Meimi.

"I don't like this Fritz," I state.

Meimi tilts her head. "I trust Fritz more than the Scythe." She exhales a long breath and hugs her elbows. Shivers rack her small frame.

"You need sleep," I say gently.

At the mention of the word *sleep*, Meimi lets out a massive yawn. "Yes, I do." She turns around. All of a sudden, we stand only a few inches apart. Our gazes meet. Seconds pass, and it's as if this factory, project and search mission all evaporate. There's only me and Meimi. I recall what I saw when we first met.

Dancing.

Tooling on hoverbikes.

Laughing.

There's so much I want to share with her, and no time for it. *Yet.*

"What about you?" asks Meimi. "Do you need to sleep?"

"I don't require much rest." Much as I'd love to chat, right now the first priority must be getting my transcendent to bed. I take a pointed step away from Meimi. "Especially when I have work to do."

"Looking for Luci?"

"Among other things. I can't do anything until my gear is ready." I need that monolith functioning and fast.

"Well, good night." Meimi steps away, pauses, and gives me a half wave.

"Sleep well."

Meimi heads off to her bedroom. Soon both her and Rose are deep asleep. After checking on Meimi, I'm ready tromp back to the basement and work on my monolith, but my sentient keep sending me images of Justice and Cole. It's obvious what they want me to do next. And although I'd rather work on that monolith, it's always best to do as my sentient command.

Which means it's time to check on my brothers.

CHAPTER 10

"No matter what the fight, ensure that many battle as one." – Wu Zhao Zetain,
The Art Of Sentient War

I STAND outside Meimi's door, summon my vision sentient, and issue a
command.

Show me Slate and Justice.

Blue particles lift from my skin, rising into a loop before me. The tiny
bits of azure whirl about. More follow until a two-dimensional whirlpool
of blue hangs in the air. Now, if I wanted to open a drift void to visit my
home planet, I could punch or walk through this circle of blue sentient.

But I don't.

Why? There's no knowing why my sentient wish me to look in on my
brothers. Opening a full drift void would expose my location. Instead, I
reach my hands into the center of the thin plate of sentient before me
and pull. This opens a view to my home world, what's called a stealth
void. Now, I can see my brothers, but they can't see me.

Perfect.

The view through the stealth void shows me the interior of the Grand
Palais. My brothers wait in one of our parlay chambers. Heavy red
curtains cover the walls, along with the occasional mirror in a gilded
frame. Chaise longue chairs decorate the space, the kind with velvet
cushions and golden frames. A great candelabra hangs from the ceiling.

Nearby, three guards stand at the ready: two men and one woman. All
of them wear long black dusters with silver stars on the lapel. Matching
pins also decorate their wide-brimmed hats.

While the guards look on, my brothers speak in low voices. It's common for us to use a parlay chamber. I step closer to the loop before me, trying to catch what they're saying.

Something else grabs my interest instead.

One of the guards becomes enveloped in a sheath of thin red lightning bolts. The nest of lines quickly encircles the figure until the image of Doc Zykin appears over the guard, all made from the same interlocking web of tiny crimson lines. The other guards notice right away.

"Your Highnesses," says one warrior. "Red sentient."

The two free guards pull gash guns from their holsters, pointing the weapons toward the altered warrior.

Turning, Justice faces the changed man as well. If the fact that Doc Zykin is appearing bothers him, then Justice doesn't show it.

"Guess I should've seen this coming," Justice drawls. He gestures to the guards. "Stand down." The warriors lower their weapons, but don't re-holster them. *Wise move.*

"Disrespectful," adds Slate.

That's a mild way of putting it. If Justice and Slate want to chat alone, then Doc Zykin should never go chasing after them, let alone possess one of their guards and use that guy as a doorway to break in on a private conversation. The fact that Zykin's doing this at all only proves how much power the doctor's gaining over Father. Even six months ago, Zykin would never have dared to interrupt my brothers.

Within seconds, the possessed guard is surrounded by a frame of thin lightning bolts that are in the exact shape of Doc Zykin. There's the tall hat, grizzled face, and goatee ... all perfectly formed by a delicate web of red and glowing cords. Once the figure is complete, the lit-up version of Doc Zykin steps away from the guard. Red light seeps across the room, casting everything in a crimson glow.

But the show's not over yet.

A burst of red brightness flares across the chamber. One moment, Zykin is a figure who's made from thin lines of lightning. The next, those bright cords have transformed into a flesh and blood. No more lightning, only Doc Zykin. It's an impressive trick, I'll give the doc that. You need to truly master red sentient in order to pull it off.

With the transformation over, the once-possessed guard crumples to the floor, unconscious. The guy will probably stay passed out for hours.

Justice nods to the other guards. "Take your comrade outside. We need to chat with the doc here."

The other warriors drag the passed-out guard from the room. Like always, the wall shimmies as they approach it, changing from the illusion of red tapestry into a panel of crimson filaments. The long strands part like a curtain, allowing the guards to take off.

And leaving my brothers alone with Doc Zykin.

Back in the factory, my gaze locks on Meimi's door. It's really tempting to step through this drift void and help my brothers. But I know Justice too well. He'd make good on his threat to put my sentient on lock-down. There's no way I'd be able to stay here and help Meimi.

Doc Zykin strokes his goatee while speaking in his classic sing-song voice. "Cole, he had three little lambs, their fleece was white as snow. But every time Doc asked to chat with them, away they're sure to go."

"We get it," says Justice. "We've been avoiding you. You want to parlay. That's what the room's for, so say your piece and get out."

"Thorny worry, pudding and pie. Hid from Doc Zykin and made him cry."

Justice sets his hands on his hips. "I hate your sing-song nonsense. Cole's not here. You don't have to put on the act."

Doc Zykin blinks innocently. "Thorny worry, pudding—"

"Fine," interrupts Justice. "We get it. You want to find Thorne. Well, we don't know where he is, Doc. Let it drop."

This is a lie, of course. I gave a false mission to the Viz Dome. Still, I appreciate the fact that Justice won't tell Doc Zykin anything. The man is a creep.

Zykin grins. "Eeny, meeny, miny, moe. Thorne caught his transcendent by the toe. Let me kill him, or down YOU'LL go. Eeny, meeny, miny, moe."

A jolt of alarm runs down my limbs. How could Zykin know about Meimi? Then I remember it. I shared my blue sentient with her when we first met. Somehow that must have caused a schism point. The Komandir are masters of both red sentient and schisms. Somehow, Doc Zykin used his powers to figure out what happened.

Justice sniffs. "Enough with this transcendent garbage. You've been trying to assassinate Thorne for years. Slate and I are not listening to you."

The nearby wall transforms from crimson curtains into a panel of shifting red filaments. The lines part and Mother steps into the room. She wears another high-necked dress made from what looks like intricate lace.

"It is time for me to address our people," explains Mother. She looks to Slate. "I shall need your knowledge and vision sentient."

Slate nods. "Always."

Every week, the royal family addresses the people of Umbra. Small drift voids open before each citizen and the royals speak to our citizens through them. Time was, Father used to do these addresses, but his speeches became unhinged. Now Mother holds them with Justice and Slate. I'm kept on the sidelines for obvious reasons. No one wants to see the weak prince.

Mother rounds on Doc Zykin. "You're excused."

"Hickory dickory dock, the doc must leave the clock." Doc Zykin bows and heads toward the wall. It opens for him, just as it did for Mother, and then closes after he's left.

Mother twists her mouth with disgust. "Horrid man. What did he want?"

"You won't believe this," says Justice. "Doc Zykin thinks Thorne found his transcendent."

Mother waves her hand dismissively. "Transcendents are a myth. Doc Zykin merely wants to upset your father." Mother focuses on Justice. "Cole is convinced that you'll soon discover your transcendent and challenge him for the throne. I've forbidden Doc Zykin from speaking of it, so that must be why he's taken to discussing Thorne instead."

Pangs of worry move across my rib cage. If what Mother says is true, then this news about Doc Zykin could place both Meimi and my brothers at even more risk.

Mother turns to Slate. "You haven't had any new visions, have you?"

"None," states Slate.

"Now I must issue new orders to keep Zykin in line," says Mother. "I swear, if your father weren't so fond of the man, then I'd have had that *nursery rhyming freak* killed ages ago." She shakes her head, as if snapping herself out of visions of murder. "Where is Thorne?"

"On a mission," answers Justice. "It's for a version of the planet Xy." The sentient home planet is a rather strange place to visit, to say the least. I'd hoped no one would try to follow me there and confirm where I really went. Good to see my plan has worked so far.

"That boy is forever running off. Most inconvenient." Mother folds her hands at her waist. "I was hoping to find all three of you, but we'll need to have this chat without Thorne."

"Not again, Ma," says Justice. My heart goes out to my brothers. I already know what Mother is about to discuss with them. She brought up the same topic with me before I left to help Meimi.

Patricide.

"Your father's losing his mind," says Mother. "He's in pain. You know what we must do."

Justice folds his arms over his chest. "Answer's still no."

Slate steps between Mother and Justice. "Address."

This is Slate's way of saying that Mother still needs to make her weekly address to the people. And to stop discussing how we must murder father.

Mother sighs. "This is only delaying the evitable."

"*Now*," adds Slate. He can be quite bossy when he sets his mind to it.

"The S-Man is right," says Justice. "We can't keep the people waiting."

"Fine," states Mother. Although her tone says that word, it's clear she really thinks things are anything but *fine*. Along with Justice and Slate, Mother steps through the wall and leaves the chamber.

Show's over.

Closing my eyes, I command my sentient to vanish. A moment later, the round plate before me dematerializes. I'm no longer watching my brothers, but I'm now more worried than ever. The fact that Doc Zykin is talking about my transcendent is serious bad news. Sure, no one's taking Doc Zykin seriously right now, but eventually, Cole will listen. He always does. Perhaps I should get to work on that monolith and see what I can discover. Maybe there's information on this world that could help me finish here quickly and return to Umbra.

Once more, my sentient have their own ideas of what should happen next. Before I step toward the basement, my sentient shoot me images of the exterior of the chemical plant, as well as pictures of Meimi's door. I address them in my mind.

You want me to guard her door?

My sentient send me images of smiling faces. That would be *yes*.

I tap my chin, considering. Actually, my sentient are absolutely right about this one. My brothers have more than enough power to take care of themselves. Meanwhile, Meimi has just as many enemies as my royal family.

Yet I'm the only one who can keep her safe.

"When meeting strangers in a parallel reality, always trust your intuition. If you suspect someone to be a rogue, you're probably correct." – Beauregard the Great, *Instructions for Visiting Parallel Worlds*

I SIT with my back against Meimi's closed bedroom door. Sickly beams of greenish moonlight reflect off my body armor. Thoughts fly through my mind. The discussion between my mother and brothers ... Doc Zykin knowing the truth about Meimi ... and the possible threat from that criminal, Fritz. There's a lot to worry about.

Of all these, my sentient are most concerned with Fritz. They keep sending me images of his square face speckled with raindrops.

"NO!" Meimi's voice echoes in from her bedroom.

Alarm rattles through my nervous system. Leaping to my feet, I burst through the door and pause, soaking in the scene. Meimi sits upright in bed, her body glistening with sweat. She yanks anxiously at the neckline of her T-shirt. I scan every corner of the room, searching for trouble. To be prepared, I summon my battle sentient to form short swords, one on each arm.

Meimi stares at me, her brown eyes wild. "What are you doing?"

"Guarding you."

"From what?"

I sniff. "Do you want an alphabetized list?"

Meimi exhales. Little by little, the edges of her sweet mouth curl into a grin. "That would help, yes."

I can't help but smile a bit myself. "Well, the letter A is for the *asshat* who took your prototype." I twist my wrists; the sentient-created swords retract into my skin. "Not sure if you can tell, but I didn't like that guy."

Meimi's smile widens. "Yeah, I got that."

We share a long look. There's a glint in Meimi's eyes. *Amazement.* Somehow I know she didn't expect me to be outside her door. Not that I blame her. Meimi has spent her whole life caring for her mother, alone.

Well, that ends now.

Going forward, she'll always have me.

Meimi pull her covers up under her chin. "Thanks for checking in. I'll just ... go back to sleep."

My transcendent looks so lost and alone. There's no way I'll leave her now. With gentle movements, I cross the room and sit beside Meimi on her tiny mattress.

"Tell me what happened." Reaching forward, I trace circles on her back with my fingertips. "Why did you scream?"

"I had a nightmare."

"What did you see?"

"I was in the kitchen downstairs with Miss Edith. The Merciless showed up. Everyone was killed. Mom too."

"Rose is safe and asleep. Miss Edith won't be here for hours. And I'll be right outside that door."

"You aren't treating this as just a dream."

"It's not." I meet her gaze. "It's a warning. My people place a lot of emphasis on dreams. And my sentient are restless, which is another danger sign. But I merged some of them with the security system. If anything comes close, I'll know."

"Ah, your alphabetized list. A is for *Asshat.*"

"B is for *Bad guys.*" I run my finger along her jawline. Meimi shivers. "You need to rest and ..." I pause. Images from my sentient appear in my mind, all of them coming from outside the factory. Shadows now move within the heavy sheets of rain. I frown.

"What's wrong?"

"Information is coming in from my sentient." I don't need to explain what that means, because Meimi's grasped my palm so tightly, her nails dig into my skin. She can already sense the truth.

Trouble is coming.

CHAPTER 12

"Current images from sentient are the windows to future success." – Wu Zhao
Zetain, *The Art Of Sentient War*

FRESH PICTURES APPEAR from my sentient. Outside the factory, humans
move under the cover of heavy rain and darkness. I focus my sentient so
I can catch both sound and images. Whispers carry through the rumble
of the rainstorm. My sentient transfer the conversation as noise only I
can detect.

"You're sure she's here?" asks one man.
　　"Ya, ya." I know the second speaker. That's Fritz. "Meimi will be inside."
　　"Anyone else?" asks the first man.
　　"No one you need worry about," answers Fritz.

My blood heats with rage. I knew that Fritz was a traitor. Meimi
squeezes my hand again, snapping me out of my thoughts. Once more, I
meet her gaze straight on. There's no point dancing around the truth.

"The Merciless are approaching the factory," I explain. "I can clearly
hear their conversation."

Meimi gasps. "Mom." Her gaze automatically shifts to the far wall.
On the other side of that partition, Rose is still sound asleep.

"No," I say gently. "They're not after her. They were talking about
you." I tilt my head, thinking things through. "Once they cross into the

factory, my systems will scan them more deeply. I'll get a better read on their plans."

Meimi's hand turns cold with fear. "The Merciless have only one plan. Shoot people."

Smash!

Downstairs in the factory, windows shatter. The security system wails a few long sirens before falling silent. Voices echo through the factory. This time, they're close enough that Meimi can hear them as well.

"Ya, ya," says Fritz. "You'll find her upstairs. Second room on the left."

Meimi gasps. "This is more than the Merciless." She sets her free hand against her throat. "Fritz and the Scythe sold me out."

Shock rattles my nervous system, but I set the emotion aside. *Think through the problem, Thorne.* Closing my eyes, I pull on my knowledge sentient, commanding them to search through the intruders. Four Merciless guards march with the group. Their mission plan appears in my mind.

Capture Target: Meimi Archer

Crime: Injuring the Merciless and Doctor Godwin at Reclamation Center RCM1

Mission: Bring her to Mass General

My thoughts race. These guards want to drag Meimi off to some hospital? I force my sentient to scan their minds again. Another report appears in my mind.

Mass General Requisition Contract

Target: Meimi Archer

Procedure: Memory wipe

My skin chills over with fear. These men plan to take Meimi to some hospital and erase her mind. I shake my head, snapping my thoughts out of the connection through my sentient. Meimi sits beside me on the bed, her lower lip trembling with a held-in sob.

"I have accessed more data," I explain. Every muscle in my body turns taut with a lethal mixture of worry and rage. I rise from the cot. "They have plans for you."

Meimi still sits in bed, her face slack with shock. Downstairs on the factory floor, a chorus of bootfalls echo, along with the click of weapons being unholstered.

They're closing in.

Meimi whips off her covers. "I have to get Mom."

"Go to Rose, and they'll shoot her just to reach you. They don't care about your mother. They won't kill you because they plan to—"

Meimi stands, placing her fingertips on my lips. "I don't want to know. All I want is for Mom to be safe. Please, Thorne. Guard her as you would me."

My heart sinks. She can't ask this. I just found my brilliant Meimi, and now I must lose her light? It's not possible.

I shake my head. "Don't ask me this."

"If there's some connection between us, you already know the truth. I won't be moved."

I search her face in the sickly moonlight. We're two figures standing in the darkness, waiting for death and separation. Yet I can't sacrifice Meimi's mind. Suddenly, an idea appears. Unfortunately, this plan means sharing my sentient with Meimi, which might tip off my father that one of his sons really has a transcendent. After all, just sharing thoughts with Meimi alerted Doc Zykin, and my father is far more powerful than that snake oil salesman.

But I simply must save Meimi.

Even if it does bring me one step closer to patricide.

Reaching forward, I cup Meimi's face in my hands. "Then let me help you in another way. Can you trust in that?"

"Yes, Thorne." Meimi's voice comes out rough and low. "I trust you."

Closing my eyes, I summon my vision sentient to the fore. Their power skitters across my skin, like cool mist on a searing hot day. For my plan to work, I must take my true form. So that's exactly what I do. When I open my eyes once again, I find Meimi staring at me, honest and unafraid.

"You're blue," she says simply.

"Yes."

"You really, really are an alien."

I smile. "And you're not frightened of me."

"I should be." Meimi's voice is a husky whisper while her gaze stays locked on my mouth.

"Never be frightened of me, Rosa Meimifloria Archer, my glorious girl named after the drift rose." I lean in closer, stopping when my warm breath fans across her sweet lips. "I'll do whatever it takes to keep you safe. And for me, my people, a kiss can connect our consciousness in special ways." I gently move my mouth across hers.

Black, silver, and blue light now flare around me. A moment later, the same colors shine from Meimi's skin as well. Deep within our souls, new links form between us. Energies entwine. Intellectual cogs connect and spin. I command my sentient to form a mental fortress around all that is truly Meimi, locking her essence down tightly until another kiss from me can release her true self. Our shared light flares more brightly, then dies down once more. All signs of sentient vanish.

The protection is in place.

Meimi breaks the kiss, breathless. "What was that?" she asks.

"The only way I can keep you safe." My mouth thins to a determined line. "Although it will mean a battle with my father."

"Over me?"

I nod.

Meimi's mouth falls open with shock. "Don't do that. I'm not worth it."

"That's where you're wrong, Meimi. You're remarkable."

"Why? Because I build prototypes?"

"No, because you've a true heart, stellar mind, and fighting spirit. I'd tear apart any number of universes for you. You may find this hard to believe, but I already have."

There's so much I want her to understand. Past, present, future ... in all of them, Meimi and I share a sacred bond. Yet though our connection is rock-solid, that doesn't mean it's unbreakable. Actions in any one universe can cause a domino affect though others. I could lose my Meimi.

Please, let this protection be enough to keep her mind whole.

Meimi scans my face carefully, as if seeing me for the first time. "Transcendent," she whispers.

I frame her beloved face with my fingertips. "That's right," I say softly.

Moving up on tiptoe, Meimi touches her mouth to mine. Our kiss quickly deepens. The sweep of her tongue across my lips heats my body with desire. Yet bootfalls sound on the metal staircase outside, interrupting us. *The Merciless.* Meimi and I break apart. I know she's thinking the same thing that I am.

That might be our last kiss.

I give Meimi a sad smile. "When the time is right, that kiss will help you remember." Stepping over to the wall, I set my hands against the concrete. "And until then, your mother will be safe."

Silver sentient shimmer on my palms. The tiny particles with spread out from my hands, creating an oval on the wall. For a heartbeat, the concrete shimmers with a metallic glow. Then an opening appears, connecting this room to Rose's chamber.

I turn to Meimi and pause. The thought is there but unspoken. *Do you really want me to leave?*

Meimi nods. *Yes.*

Steeling my shoulders, I step through the newly-made exit and into Rose's bedroom. She lays atop the covers, deep asleep. Behind me, the concrete returns to its regular gray.

I set my hands against the wall once more. As I did with my brothers, I open a stealth void to the next room. If my guess is right, they'll come to Meimi before going after Rose.

If I'm to save my transcendent, I simply must see what happens next.

CHAPTER 13

"Even when facing a mundane-looking the mission, always be ready for surprise." –
Beauregard the Great, *Instructions for Visiting Parallel Worlds*

I SET my palms against the concrete. Once again I summon my silver
sentient. The gray wall shimmers as a metallic oval appears on the
concrete. I place my hands into the center, grip hard, and pull. As my
hands draw apart, I create a round window into Meimi's room. Now I
can see and hear everything, but no one can tell that I'm watching. The
first thing I witness is Fritz stomping across the threshold, followed by
four Merciless warriors. He gestures toward Meimi. "That's her, ya."

Bands of worry tighten across my chest. Every instinct I have tells me
to rush back into Meimi's room and protect her. But I gave her my word.
Glancing over my shoulder, I watch Rose's sleeping form. She's little
more than a skeleton curled up onto her side. This woman sacrificed so
much to keep her daughters safe.

Meimi is right.

Rose can't be killed.

Somehow, I'll protect them both.

For her part, Meimi glares at Fritz. "So you're pawning me off to the
Merciless. How could you?"

"There was just too much money in it." Fritz drops his false accent.
"The things you can do, Meimi. You've gotten too big for even me and
the Scythe to control."

Memories appear. Earlier today, Meimi fabricated quantum tools
from piles of worthless junk. She's remarkable. Clearly, that's what the
government wants. Her gifts.

One of the Merciless steps forward, but Fritz holds out his arm, stopping the warrior in his tracks. "Let me explain things to her. It will go more easily that way." Fritz steps closer to my transcendent. "The Authority is taking you, but don't worry. You're far too valuable to be killed."

"And my mother?" asks Meimi.

"You already know the answer to that question, Meims. Once we're done with you, we'll euthanize her. That should have happened long ago."

Fritz reaches behind him. When his arm comes back out, he's holding a syringe with blue liquid. I saw that in the briefing visions from the Merciless. That vial is filled with tranquilizer.

Meimi still glares at the hulking man. "We had a deal."

"A deal means equal parties, Meimi." Fritz's eyes soften with sadness. "That's never how it was with us." He snaps his fingers, and four Merciless guards leap toward Meimi, holding her in place. Fritz plunges the syringe into her neck and pushes down the plunger.

I grip the concrete wall, my fingers tearing through the stone. They're drugging my Meimi.

No, no, no.

Meimi's eyes start rolling into back her head. Blinking hard, she refocuses on Fritz. My transcendent is a fighter.

"Nice try," she snarks.

"Because you think you're immune," says Fritz. "But not from this level of dose."

Meimi gasps and frowns. All her bravado disappears. Which means one thing. *She'll pass out soon.* On reflex, I firm my grip on the wall. More solid concrete turns to dust in my palms.

"Don't worry, Meims." Fritz has the balls to smile. "When the Merciless are done, you'll have a new identity, memory, sponsor family, everything. This will be better for you. Rose was holding you down."

Meimi blinks slowly. Clearly, it's an effort for her to stay awake. A man steps into the room. With an exaggerated swoop of her head, Meimi turns to face him. This man appeared in my sentient visions as well.

Doctor Godwin.

He's a little man with a balding head and small round glasses. A white lab coat hangs loosely on his small frame. Godwin raises a briefcase in his hands. And not just any briefcase, it's the one holding the prototype that Meimi and I just created. "Did you build this?"

Meimi's head wobbles as she speaks. "No."

"Don't listen to her," counters Fritz. "That thing is set for her high school and it's covered in her DNA. It's like I told you right after the massacre at RCM1. Meimi is brilliant. She can get you what you need. You saw what she did at RCM1."

Another sentient memory appears. There was something about RCM1 on the mission briefing for the Merciless warriors. Meimi faced down Godwin and some goons at RCM1. That must be why this doctor is so set on controlling her.

"I only witnessed a petulant child who knows how to toss a chem dart," says Godwin.

"So?" counters Fritz. "That's why we sent you the enhancer as proof. But you still weren't convinced. Which is why Meimi built you this prototype in less than a day." Fritz folds his arms over his chest. "It's pretty clear to me that she's what you need. Or are you just sore that she knocked you out at RCM1? Big bad doctor getting dosed with tranqs?"

"I'm not sore." Godwin's nostrils flare. "I do need a drift scientist."

"Like I said, that's Meimi," declares Fritz.

My breathing slows a bit. Much as I don't trust Fritz, I must admit he's trying to help Meimi. That fact might come in handy later on.

"We'll see," says Godwin in a sinister whisper. "I need to see her perform in a controlled environment over time. No tricks. Bring in her sponsors."

A couple steps into Meimi's bedroom. "Meet your new charge," Godwin says to the pair. "You'll sponsor her for the summer. If her work pleases me, she can attend ECHO Academy. I might even bring her into my full plans."

The woman turns to face Meimi. Shock and rage course through me, all at once. I've seen that face before.

It's Meimi's sister, Luci.

The woman looks just like the images I saw before: white-blonde hair, thin frame, and icy blue eyes. Essentially, a female version of Truman Archer. She glares at Meimi with a look of pure hatred.

"I told you already," snaps Luci. "Meimi can't help you with drift science. She's useless."

Meimi's stood upright all this time, despite the drugs. For the first time, she stumbles backward, her face slack with shock. The back of her legs slam against her cot. She collapses into a seated position.

My poor Meimi. She never suspected her sister was behind this. Neither did I, for that matter. I have my own family issues, sure. That said, my siblings are my rocks of stability in a fast-moving torrent of threats.

Godwin rounds on Meimi's sister. "What part of my instructions were unclear?"

Luci frowns. "But—"

"Don't test me, Luci. You're only here because you're her sister and every other attempt we've made to recruit this girl has failed. We ask her to volunteer at school? She's not interested. The Scythe asks to be her sponsor? He gets turned down. Now it's up to you two." He eyes Luci from head to toe. "You and your husband are the worst sponsor parents in our system. Do you want to keep the credits rolling in? Fix this."

I make mental notes to research all this later on, from the sponsor parent system to this place called ECHO Academy. Any information might help later on.

Luci stomps her foot. "I already told you, Meimi can't do it."

"You better hope she can," says Godwin. "Or you'll pay the price." He glares at the man. "You too, Josiah."

For the first time, the man beside Luci speaks. "Hey, she's not *my* sister."

"My threat goes for both of you." Godwin stares at the Merciless guards. For a moment, I think he might order them to fire on Luci. Instead, Godwin slides the briefcase under his arm and marches out of the room.

Now, it's Josiah who turns around to face Meimi. He reminds me of a modern version of Doc Zykin. Uneven features. Overly greased back hair. Cheap frayed suit. Josiah scans Meimi with what can only be described as a leer. "You've grown up."

Protective instincts zoom through every cell in my body. I'm about to punch through the wall—and then Josiah's face—when Meimi turns to Luci. Every inch of my transcendent's face is tight with rage. "Why are you doing this?"

Even drugged and afraid, my transcendent fights.

Luci doesn't reply, only stalks closer. "Dad loved roses, you know that? It all started because Mom's name is Rose. Then he named me after the white rose, Luciae. You're named after the drift rose, Meimifloria."

Meimi's eyes flutter once more. The drugs are really hitting her now. She crumples onto her side. The sight makes my heart crack.

My fierce woman.

A pure transcendent.

Drugged and fading.

"And for a while, our family's life was nothing but roses, too," continues Luci. "That is, until *you* came along. Dad used to make good money. Mom did, too. We were set until *you* ruined everything. But now, things are finally turning around. Godwin's setting you up, and I'll be the beneficiary. And the best part? You'll have your memory wiped, so you won't recall any of this conversation."

Meimi stares at her evil sister with a look that can only be described as total disbelief. I decide I'll hold to my mission of finding Luci. That said, there are no guarantees of what I'll do once she's located.

Luci looms over Meimi's bed and grins. "You'll repay your debt to me, Pumpkin. I'll make sure of it."

Meimi's eyes flutter shut. *She's gone.* A roar of pain tears from my lungs.

Fierce.

Primal.

Unstoppable.

"What's that, ya?" asks Fritz. He points to the Merciless guards and then the door. "Check it out."

The warriors rush over to Rose's room. At the same time, I scoop Meimi's mother from the bed, open a drift void to Umbra, and kick the silver connection between this world and my home.

Both Rose and I are gone before the Merciless open the door.

CHAPTER 14

"We Umbrans inhabit a large planet, yet through filament technology, we can monitor each other easily." – Empress Janais, *The Fifth Age of Umbra*

I STEP through drift void and onto a stretch of Umbra's Charcoal Mountains. The area I've entered sits at the bottom of a steep crevasse. All around me, gray rock juts up toward a pale blue sky. There's nothing green or growing as far as the eye can see. In some ways, it reminds me of versions of reality where humans colonize the moon.

A small ranch house lays nestled in the deepest part of the valley. There's no one else around for miles. The building is a one-story affair made of stout round rocks held together with heavy masonry. An arched wooden roof tops the structure.

Here it is.

Truman Archer's home.

Rose groans in my arms. I firm my hold on her and whisper. "You'll feel better soon, I swear." I stomp up the main steps. "Come out, Truman!"

The front door opens a crack. I see a sliver of Truman's face. His skin seems to hang loose on his high cheekbones. That said, his eyes still shine bright blue. He's sharp as ever, this one.

He spies me, gasps, and falls down on his knees. "Prince Thorne."

"Please rise," I state. I don't add what everyone else on Umbra knows. People bow to my brothers, not to me. Truman must not get around much.

But Truman doesn't rise. He stays kneeling and with his head bowed. "Is Janais with you?" he asks.

Now, I knew Mother checked in on Truman from time to time. After all, the man did our family a great service and he lives an isolated life. That said, I don't like the fact that they're on a first name basis. At all.

I narrow my eyes. "You mean her Royal Highness, the Empress of Umbra?"

"Yes, excuse me. Her Royal Highness." Finally, Truman stands. He wears human clothes: khakis and a white collared shirt. After he fully opens the door, all the color drains from his face. "Rose." Truman looks at me, his eyes wide with shock. "What happened?"

"She's been on your Earth too long. You need to hide her. Her mind will recover if she remains on Umbra."

"Rose." Truman's blue eyes line with tears. He looks ready to fall over himself. This isn't going well.

"Can you focus?" I ask.

Truman pulls up his glasses and rubs his eyes. The motion seems to help him. "Yes."

"Then listen to me carefully," I say, my voice low. "Your wife isn't even supposed to be on Umbra. No one can know she's here. Even my mother."

Truman resets his glasses. There's a too-long pause before he speaks again. "Let's get her inside."

"Not until I have your vow."

"My what?"

"Your solemn promise," I state. "I brought your wife here because I thought you would keep her from harm. Yet I can't help but notice how you won't commit that to me clearly. If you can't protect Rose, then say so. I'll figure out something else."

Sadly, I've no idea what that will be. Although it wouldn't be my first time making things up as I go. It always works out in the end.

"No," says Truman quickly. "That's not what I meant. Rose is my heart. My life. I will protect her with everything in me, I swear it."

I nod toward the door. "Then lead on. It isn't safe to keep standing out here."

"Right." Truman steps back, allowing me to enter his home. Inside, the place is all natural wooden floors and open spaces. Truman's brought together a neat mixture of Earther conveniences. Like I said, the man won't use filament technology. Not that I blame him. Filaments are easily tracked. If you want real privacy, use old Earther stuff. I should know. I have an entire warehouse full of Earther items that I use for different missions. I may not have sentient, but I do get the gear.

"Where should I place her?" I ask.

"Guest bedroom." Truman crosses a thin hallway and opens the first door. Inside, the room is all gauzy white curtains and lots of light. I set Rose stop the wide bed.

Truman nibbles at his thumb. "Her Royal Highness won't like this."

I round on Meimi's father. "I don't know what that means and I don't want to know. All that's important is how Rose stays safe. Again, if you can't protect her, just say so right now. This is your last chance. I won't ask again."

In all honesty, I'm not pleased I had to ask twice to begin with.

"Rose will be safe, I swear it." The guy looks both terrified and elated. I suppose that will have to do. If I linger here too long, I could lose track of where they place Meimi. Just because they said they'd take her to Mass General doesn't mean that's where she'll end up. I've seen too many missions go sideways to trust that things will work out the way I expect.

"In that case, excuse me."

Truman grabs my elbow. "You were ... at my planet of origin?"

"Yes."

"How are Luci and Meimi?"

Before, I might have been tempted to tell Truman all about his daughters. Perhaps I might have even shared that Meimi is my transcendent. But after all that talk about Janais, I'm not saying more than I absolutely have to. At least, not until I fully understand what's going on.

"They are well," I say simply. "I'm protecting them."

Over on the bed, Rose's eyes flutter open. "Truman," she whispers. "The accident. Too much Crown Sentient in your mind. All my fault."

Truman rushes to sit beside her, taking her hand in his. "You're here now. I'll take care of you."

"And I'll take my leave." I don't wait for any more chatter or grabbing of elbows. I make my way out the door.

The last thing I hear as I depart is Truman calling after me.

"Thank you."

"Just keep your word, Truman. That's the best way to show appreciation."

CHAPTER 15

"Sentient are your eyes and ears on the omniverse." – Hammurabi the Seventh, *Law of Sentient*

ONCE I'M outside the ranch house, I close my eyes and summon my sentient.

Take me to Mass General under the New Boston Dome.

A moment passes.

Two.

Nothing happens.

Instead, my sentient send me images of avalanches and cave-ins. Frustration tightens my throat. No question what this means; it's happened before on other missions.

Is something blocking you? I ask in my mind.

More images appear. This time they are of people nodding, *yes.*

Are you locked out of the dome or the entire continent?

A satellite-style picture enters my mind. It's a high-up view of a crystalline dome set into an otherwise dreary landscape. Which means my sentient work on the continent, just not in the dome.

Odd, but every world has its quirks.

I pace a line in the muck outside the ranch house and think things through. Not being able to use my sentient is rough, but not impossible. In most of my missions, I bring extra supplies to compensate my low powers. And there's one place I keep all those goodies. I summon my sentient once more.

Take me to Warehouse Nine.

A loop of silver forms in the air before me. Leaving the Charcoal

Mountains, I step through the drift void and into a spot on the other side of Umbra. It's a darkened place with tall ceiling and row after row of shelves. My secret warehouse. Like Truman's home, everything here is filament-free. Human stuff, mostly. Although I do have some supplies from missions on Xy, the sentient's home planet. The moment I step out across the concrete floor, fluorescent lights flare to life overhead. I make a mental list of what I'll need.

Hoverbike.

Human clothes.

Computer hacking equipment.

Marching down the aisles, I gather up my supplies. In short order, I've packed my gear into the saddlebags on my hoverbike. Mounting the machine, I get ready to open a drift void for Meimi's world.

That's when a loop of silver sentient appears in front of me.

Trouble is, it's not of my creation.

As I dismount my hoverbike, my hands curl into fists. Who found out that I'm back in Umbra? Cole? Doc Zykin?

A moment later, Justice and Slate step through the silver void. Once they're safely in my warehouse, the circle of particles disappears behind them. My mind races. Justice said he'd put me on lock down if I tried to help Rose. And here I am, doing just that.

This isn't great.

"Interesting place," drawls Justice.

I keep my demeanor carefully neutral. "It's where I store stuff for missions."

"Big," comments Slate.

Justice purses his lips. "Were you ever gonna tell us about this?"

"Which part?" I ask. "My warehouse or leaving Umbra?"

"Everything," says Slate.

I frown. *Here it comes.* "No on both counts. The fewer people who know about this warehouse, the less likely it will ever be discovered. And as for leaving on another mission, you know I come and go on my own schedule. You saw the mission record in the Viz Dome, right?"

"This time, it's not so simple," says Justice. "Doc Zykin has kicked up his plans for you. And by plans, I mean he wants to kill you. Came up with this cockamamie story about you finding your transcendent. So I did some digging with my sentient. Turns out, you went to help Rose Archer, didn't you?"

"I did."

"And?" asks Slate. The gleam in his eyes says he knows what's coming next, or suspects it.

"Don't torture the guy," says Justice. "He hasn't found his transcendent. We just got worried you would get yourself killed helping Rose. Plus, Doc Zykin was acting so weird."

Slate steps closer, his gaze turning intense "And?" he asks me again.

Justice pauses. A heavy silence hangs in the warehouse. At last, I break the quiet.

"Doc Zykin was right. I've found my transcendent. I'm returning to her Earth to protect her right now." While I'm at it, I figure I better tell them everything. "She's Rose Archer's daughter, Meimi."

Justice whips off his Stetson and tosses it on the floor. "What in the ever loving hell? You were supposed to be on Xy."

I keep my features steady. "I lied."

"No kidding. Damn it all, Thorne! I gave my word I'd put you on lock-down. You went once, that's fine and dandy. But I can't let you sneak off twice. Now what am I gonna do?"

Slate steps closer, pausing when we're face to face. I'm worried that he'll pull out a syringe and actually inject me with the lock-down drug, but he does something completely different instead. Reaching forward, Slate wraps me in a deep hug. "Transcendent," he says, his voice low with awe.

"What is wrong with you, Slate?" asks justice. "You know we can't let him go back to her."

Slate rounds on Justice. My brother isn't one to show emotion, but right now? Every line of his body can be described with one word. *Fierce.* "Transcendent," he repeats.

Now, I do love my brothers. But I can honestly say I've never cared more for Slate than I do in this moment. Stepping to his side, I rest my hand on his shoulder. "What will you do, Justice? Inject us both?"

Justice scrubs his palms over his face and mumbles long string of cuss words. I catch a *damn* and *asshole* in there. "All right, fine. You go protect your girl." Justice looks to Slate, who's still glaring daggers. "I get it. Finding your transcendent is a big deal. I overreacted."

"I don't blame you," I say. "If Cole finds out about my transcendent, it won't be easy on you both."

Justice rolls his eyes. "If Cole doesn't like his shampoo, it ain't easy on us both."

"You know what I mean," I counter.

Clearing his throat, Justice waves toward my hoverbike. "And you need all this Earther stuff ... why?"

In Justice-speak, that's his way of telling me the subject is closed. I'll go help Meimi and my brothers can deal with my father. They really are the best.

I step over to my hoverbike. "I always take extra gear, you know that." I never take this much gear, but I won't point that part out. It was tough enough to get Justice to agree to this mission in the first place.

"Sync," says Slate. It's something he often says before I leave on a mission. It means Slate wants to know when I'll check in next.

"Keep your earpieces handy. I'll reach out in a few days with a place and time where we can meet on Meimi's version of Earth."

"Good," says Slate.

Justice sighs. "Then you're really set on this?"

"I am."

"But what if Doc Zykin tracks you down on this mission?" asks Justice. "Zykin already figured out about your transcendent. Can you handle Doc alone?"

"I have before," I say.

"Not like this," counters Justice. "It's different with this transcendent stuff. He really means it this time."

I huff out a frustrated breath. "Look, I can't hang around worrying about everything that could go wrong. If they move my transcendent before I get back, I might not be able to find her again." I remount my hoverbike. "It's just another mission, that's all. Saving planets and people. It's what I do."

Justice resets his Stetson in his head. It's his move when making an emperor-style proclamation. "In that case, you aren't running off alone. Slate and I will go with you. We all have to protect her."

Now, I understand why Justice worries. He's losing Dad. Placing me at risk feels like too much. But Justice can't watch over me anymore. In fact, he hasn't been able to for a long time. I'm about to say exactly that when Slate steps forward.

Slate gently sets his hand against Justice's shoulder. "His." There's a world of explanation in that single word, and I appreciate it to the bottom of my heart.

"Slate is right," I say gently. "Meimi is mine to protect. I can do this."

Once more, Justice takes to mumbling under his breath. I catch the words *assassin* and *death*. "Two days, brother."

"Two days," I repeat.

Then, I open another drift void, rev my hoverbike, and drive straight through.

Meimi, I'm on my way.

CHAPTER 16

"When returning to a parallel world, always select a familiar point of entry." – Beauregard the Great, *Instructions for Visiting Parallel Worlds*

MY BIKE SLAMS through the loop of silver sentient before me. One moment, I'm on Umbra. The next, I'm driving up a broken asphalt road to the Ozymandias Chemical Plant.

Time to finish that monolith. At last.

My bike tears through the greenish puddles that line the road. I tool up to what should be the building's side door. It's gone, though. Now, there's only a massive hole torn in the brick wall. The sole sign off all the security systems I created are a few wires dangling from what's left of the doorframe. My heart wilts at the sight. The torn wall reminds me of a blasted solider on a battlefield. Dead.

Which is true, in a way. This building used to be full of life, what with Meimi, Rose and Miss Edith. It already feels like an empty ruin.

Parking my hoverbike, I step up to the shattered doorway. Setting my hand onto the exposed wires, I reach out for the knowledge sentient that I'd set into the system. A buzz along my fingertips tells me they're still around.

Good.

I'm pulling them back inside my body when a voice sounds behind me.

"What the hell is this?"

Wheeling around, I see Miss Edith. In all the excitement, I'd forgotten all about her. "The Merciless were here," I reply.

Miss Edith sets her hand on her throat. "What happened to Rose and Meimi?"

"They're safe," I reply. "But you should get out of here."

"I'm undesirable. Too old, you know. I must stay off grid." She pulls her frayed housecoat more tightly around her. "But that's pricy. I needed this job to stay hidden."

Stepping over to my hoverbike, I root around inside the saddlebags. These things are packed up tight, so it takes me a minute. Eventually, I find what I was looking for. Turning to Miss Edith, I offer her a small velvet sack. "You don't need a job any more."

Miss Edith takes the tiny bag and pulls it open. "Diamonds?"

"You know how to fence those without attracting attention?"

"I do."

"Good. Then leave here and never return. Meimi and Rose are safe, but they're also targets for the government. Keep a low profile and you'll be fine."

Miss Edith tilts her head. "Who are you, really?"

I debate lying, but after so many missions, you get a feel for who you can trust.

"I'm Prince Thorne Oxblood from the Planet Umbra. I fight inter-dimensional disasters."

For a long moment, Miss Edith only stares at me, her eyes narrowed. At last, she speaks. "Good. Just keep watching over Meimi and we'll get along fine."

I can't help but smile. *Miss Edith is feisty.* "What? The diamonds didn't buy your loyalty?"

She wags her finger at me. "You can't afford me, kid." With that, Miss Edith turns and stomps away through the asphalt, puddles and garbage. I watch her leave and shake my head. *Got to love Miss Edith.*

It takes some time, but I unpack the supplies I need and drag them down to Meimi's basement workplace. I won't lie. The workshop now feels laden with sadness and memories. Was it less than twenty-four hours ago that Meimi and I built a prototype here? It's certainly that long by the clock, but my heart feels as if ages have passed. Even worse, being in this place makes my soul ache. I never knew I had a transcendent, but now that I've met her? My world feels hollow without her.

All the more reason to fix this monolith.

Now that I have the right supplies, I get the monolith working in short order. From there, it doesn't take long to start hacking into government systems. Inside the tall black monolith, lights blink as my supercomputer breaks through the security protocols around the Mass General mainframe. I stand nearby, watching the small screen of my datapad for results. I don't see anything for Meimi Archer, but that's to be expected. Godwin's too smart to use her real name. That said, I do find some info on ECHO academy. That's where a new program was just installed to protect the Boston Dome.

The quantum blocker protocol.

It's a simple set of code, but it's what's locking out all my sentient when under the dome. I scan more information on the blocker. A final test run is scheduled for tomorrow morning. Interesting, but it's not Meimi.

At last, fresh data comes in from Mass General. It's about a girl called Wisteria Roberts who's been in experimental surgery for hours. Doc Godwin is her managing physician. My pulse speeds.

That has to be Meimi.

The thought makes my stomach churn. Right now, someone is wiping away Meimi's memory. I can only hope my sentient keep her true self safe. Even then, I still have to get her out of the Boston Dome. Anxiety empties all thoughts from my mind. Blinking hard, I try to focus.

Think through the problem, Thorne.

More data appears. There's a guard assigned to Wisteria. Captain Vargas. I research the guy, and it turns out he works for General Humboldt, who appears to be Doc Godwin's arch-enemy. Both Godwin and Humboldt serve President Hope, and it was the President who assigned Vargas to Meimi.

That settles it. I want Vargas's job. The only question is ... how do I get it?

Hours fly by as I hack through loads of information on Vargas, Godwin and Mass General. Little by little, a plan forms. Godwin will be attending a hospital fundraiser tonight. I break into even more systems and secure myself an invitation.

With any luck, I'll become Meimi's new guard before midnight strikes. And if I'm incredibly fortunate, I'll be able to do it without Doc Zykin following me to this version of Earth.

Probably a long shot, but a guy can hope.

CHAPTER 17

"One does the strangest things in the name of transcendence." – Empress Ophelia,
The Lost Book Of Transcendence

I STAND in the doorway to the Thirtieth Century Club on Mass Avenue.
Ladies in long gowns step by, as do guys in tuxedos. I'm on duty, checking
access wristbands on one side of the door. Another guy, Mervin, does the
same on the opposite side. Mervin's a brick wall of a man with red hair
and stubby arms. He's also obsessed with rules. Not my favorite personality type on a regular day, but this is no standard time. Meimi is trapped
somewhere under this dome, and I need to find her, fast.

"You're wearing the wrong pants," says Mervin for the seventh time. I
ignore him, so he just keeps talking. "Those are jeans. You're supposed to
wear black khakis."

At this point, I'm frustrated as hell about three things. First, that
Doc Godwin hasn't showed up yet, which means I still have to work the
entrance with Mervin. Second, I haven't gotten any new information on
Meimi since I found her alias—Wisteria Roberts—checked into Mass
general. Is she safe? Did she survive their crazy procedure?

And three, being under this dome means I can't access my sentient.
It's beyond frustrating.

Mervin still stares at me pointedly, so I suppose I need to answer him.

"I already checked in at the hostess station and ... oh, look!" I sarcas-
tically gesture across my person. "I have both my access badge—" I tap
the plastic card key at my waist "—as well as a new shirt from Shirley the
hostess." Specifically, Shirley gave me a collared garment with the Mass

Gen Security logo on the sleeve. "My pants are one hundred percent fine. You need to move on."

A muscle ticks along Mervin's jaw. "Where's Fred anyway?"

Oh, you mean Fred, the guy I erased from the duty roster for tonight?

"No idea," I say.

That said, I did give Fred a spot bonus to make up for the lost work. I'm an inter-dimensional hacker, not an asshole.

At last, Doc Godwin steps toward the door. He's a wispy man who's about five feet tall whose tuxedo hangs loosely around him.

At last.

One step closer to Meimi.

As Godwin passes, I turn to Mervin once more. "I'll just go check with Shirley again, just to be sure." Mervin looks especially relieved.

But I don't go anywhere near the hostess station. Instead, I stride up to Doc Godwin. His online profile says he appreciates aggression. "May I see your access wrist cuff?" I ask him.

Godwin gives me a double-take. "Don't you know who I am?"

"Yes. You're the man being forced to take a certain Captain Vargas as a guard."

Godwin pulls me aside. "How did you find out about Vargas?" His face almost glows with interest.

"Because I know how to get things done. In this case, I want a better job. You're the power behind President Hope. Everyone knows that. Give me Vargas's role. I'm a damned good guard and I'll be loyal to you." I hold up a data stick. "All my information is on here."

Godwin moves to take the data stick, then pauses. "I can't get rid of Vargas."

"Unless you catch him breaking the law."

Godwin sniffs. "Like that will ever happen."

"If you want it to take place, sir, I'll make it happen."

Godwin tilts his head. "Falsely accuse the Merciless and you'll end up dead."

"Nothing of value comes without risk." I press the data stick onto Godwin's hand. "It's all in there. My history. And Vargas's."

"What do you mean?"

"Vargas got unapproved body mods. Speed. Eyesight. Other stuff."

Godwin sniffs. "Everyone does that."

"He misappropriated government funds to do it."

Godwin lifts his brows. "Really? That's serious."

"Check the data stick. It's all there."

Godwin curls his hand around the data. I could shout for joy. "All right, boy. If this frames up Vargas for me, then you'll be my personal guard."

"No, I want in on whatever you're doing at Mass General. Right now."

"You *are* crafty. Fine." He sets the data stick in his pocket. "Is your DNA on this?"

"Yes." *A version of it.*

"Get rid of Vargas for me, and you'll be approved for Mass Gen. I'm a man of my word."

And with that, my trap is set. That's all the information I could scrounge up on short notice. It has to be enough to get rid of Vargas and put me in his place. If not, it'll be tough to explain why I keep showing up at Meimi's hospital.

"I wish to start tomorrow morning," I demand.

Godwin purses his lips, but doesn't respond. A pang of worry moves through me. *Was this too aggressive?* I could have sent this information via proxy. Now, Godwin has seen my face and has my cover story on a data stick. It's an effort, but I keep my features level. The worst thing that can happen now is for Godwin to see me worry.

Seconds pass. My heart beats with such force, there's a whoosh of blood in my ears. On reflex, I reach out to my sentient for information and insight.

No response.

It takes a moment for me to remember the truth. I'm in the Boston Dome and locked away from my powers.

Please, let this work.

At last, Godwin laughs. "You're a crafty one."

Not sure if that's a *yes* or a *no*, but I'll press for agreement anyway. I hold up my card key. "So authorize me right now. You can do it with your smart watch. I'll be your new guard. Done."

"I could." Godwin eyes me from head to toe. "But I won't."

A long pause follows. I don't say a word. One thing you learn in my family, and that's when someone is testing you. Godwin's doing that right now. He's waiting to see if I'll beg or whine.

If I didn't beg or whine any of the times Dad busted my jawbone, I won't do it now.

Godwin doesn't know fear.

So I keep my face still as stone. If this scheme doesn't work, I'll figure out something else. I always do. Still, beads of sweat roll down my spine. Every second I waste is another moment Meimi could be in trouble.

At last, Godwin breaks the silence. "Your charge is one Wisteria

Roberts. She'll be in the secured post-op ward." He pats his pocket. "And I'll check your data stick tonight. If it's good, that card key of yours will give you access to Mass General as of six o'clock tomorrow morning. Locate Wisteria and keep an eye on her. I'll find you when I'm ready."

"Thank you."

"Not too fast. If you don't check out, I'll send one of my attack animals after you." Godwin's voice lowers to a sinister whisper. "They'll only be able to ID your body from the blood spatters on the wall. Do we understand each other?"

"Absolutely." I bow slightly. "I'd expect nothing less from someone of your caliber." *Dirtbag.*

Godwin waves his hand. "Dismissed."

As I saunter off, a burst of elation moves through me, followed by a sobering thought.

It's a long wait until 6 am. By that time, anything could happen to Meimi.

CHAPTER 18

"Select your allies with care, then trust them with abandon. Half-measures only breed partial allegiance." – Empress Janais, *The Fifth Age of Umbra*

NEXT MORNING, 5:59 AM.

I stand in the corner of reception atrium for Mass General Hospital. Glass walls tower above me, revealing the false sunny sky of the Boston Dome. A grumpy-faced guard with sleepy eyes and long jowls sits behind the security desk. I check my watch.

6 AM on the nose.

I hand over my key card. "Thorne Oxblood, reporting for duty."

"Is that a regulation outfit?" asks the guard.

What is it with this planet and dress codes? For the record, I'm still in my jeans and security shirt from last night. For now, it's the best disguise I've got.

"Absolutely," I lie. "New rules from Godwin."

"Oh, that's fine, I suppose." The man raises his shaking hand, takes my plastic card, and inserts it into the reader on his desktop. The machine whirs softly.

Please, let this work.

His heavy brows lift. "You're approved for the experimental ward."

It's an effort not to look relieved as I take back my card. "Where is it?"

The guard smacks his thin lips together. "You sure you want to go there? Lots of strange stuff in that ward. Guards go in and they don't come back."

His words are meant to frighten me, but I find them more frustrating than anything else. In this moment, I'd love to have my sentient send me a mental schematic for this building. That way, I could just take off and leave this guy behind. Instead, I must be patient.

"I work for Doctor Godwin," I say calmly. "Believe me, I've seen everything. The experimental ward doesn't frighten me. Which way?"

The guard shrugs. "Down the right hallway, last door on the left. That's Security Checkpoint Three."

"Meaning there's two more afterwards?"

"Oh yeah. Good luck, kid." The way he says those words, it's as if I won't like those three checkpoints. But that doesn't matter. I'll do whatever it takes to reach Meimi.

I follow the guard's directions. Checkpoint Three is a small white room with a single guard and a small cart of equipment to test my identity. I give retinal and thumb scans. The guard does a finger prick, blood sample and DNA check. I'm even asked my address and the name of my first car. Everything matches the data on my identity stick. I'm waved through.

The Checkpoint Two is larger. More machines. More tests. Total time suck. I make a note to find the back doors for this place later on. They're always a bunch, if you know where to look.

At last, I hit the largest room of them all. Checkpoint One. A nurse sits behind a long white desk. He's a young guy with pale skin, dark hair, heavy glasses, and a white jumpsuit. He wears the wary frown of someone who must deal with cheats and conmen all day long. I scan the name badge.

Nurse Oakes.

Behind him, the entire wall is covered in silver machines loaded with readouts galore. A thick metal door is set into the center of it all, complete with a small viewing hole.

Is this it? Have I reached Meimi at last?

It takes everything in me not to rush past the nurse and peer through the window. Instead, I force myself to stand straight and tall. "Good morning, Nurse Oakes. I'm the new guard for Doctor Godwin."

He adjusts his heavy glasses. "You're supposed to be in body armor."

That's a bit of a surprise. Body armor? What are they doing out here, exactly? I don't want any more hold-ups, so I roll my eyes. "It's on back order. You know."

Nurse Oakes leans back in his chair. No reply.

So, not a chatty guy. Fine, as long as he lets me see Meimi.

"Do you want my key card?" I prompt.

Nurse Oakes purses his lips before swiping the card from my palm.

Rising and turning, Oakes run my card it through various inputs on the equipment wall. Things beep. Other machines hum. Before, I was able to follow every test. Now, it's hard to focus. Nervous energy thrums through my veins.

I simply must take a look.

While Oakes is busy with my key card, I step closer to the window hole. *There she is. Meimi.* No one else is in the small white chamber, just my transcendent. She lies on a silver gurney, her head wrapped in bandages. Tubes connect her nose and mouth to another wall of equipment. I scan the readouts.

Breathing.

Pulse.

Brain function.

All of it looks normal.

My first impulse is to cheer, but I tamp it down. Instead, I lean my forehead against the window instead.

Meimi's here.

Safe.

And I'm her guard.

This can work.

A familiar voice sounds behind me. "A tisket, a tasket, Prince Thorne in a casket."

A chill of alarm rolls up my back. I'd know that voice anywhere.

Doc Zykin.

Turning around, I see Nurse Oakes is already surrounded in a thin haze of red lightning bolts. I race forward, my fist cocked and ready to punch.

If I can catch Doc Zykin before he breaks through, I can end this, fast.

I swoop my arm toward the crimson figure, but at the last second, Doc Zykin steps away from Oakes. The nurse falls to the ground, unconscious. Now Doc Zykin is here and in the flesh.

This isn't good.

I lift my hands, palms forward. "I'm not going to fight you."

Mostly because I don't have my sentient here.

Or do I? Images appear in my mind. It's a replay of the last time I fought Doc Zykin back in my mission with Emma. My sentient are back ... but how?

That's when I remember it. The quantum block system was scheduled for testing this morning. Part of the plan was to bring the system down for a time. And that's when Doc Zykin decides to track me to this universe.

That's what you call shitty luck.

"Not going to punch me?" asks Doc Zykin. "Really? Because that fist heading toward my face seemed rather ominous."

My eyes widen. "You can—"

"Talk normally? Always. I simply play the fool because it pleases Cole. And I have a natural aptitude for rhymes." He grins, showing off a chipped front tooth. "Let's chat a bit, shall we?"

"What do you want?"

"I should think it's obvious. Justice won't challenge Cole to become Emperor. You will. And I'd like us to come to an understanding. I can help you gain the Crown Sentient, but you need to guarantee my place in the palace."

On reflex, I pull on my ear. *I couldn't have heard that correctly.* "Did you just say I'm going to become Emperor?"

Doc Zykin gestures toward the closed door. "You're got a transcendent."

"Meimi is human. I'm not getting more sentient. I'll never be able to challenge father."

Doc Zykin chuckles. "Who told you that? Cole did. His mind is warped. He can't even keep track of which version of Earth is the prime strain anymore. But I can see things while he's blind. You figure out how to finish missions where Umbrans with miles of Sentient have failed. It's not about what you have, it's about who you are, remember?"

The words ricochet through my soul.

It's not about what you have, it's about who you are.

Doc Zykin's grin widens. "You remember now, don't you? Your father used to say that to you. Before the Crown Sentient got to him."

It is something Dad used to say, but that's all the more reason to end this conversation. "I'm not making any deals with you to kill Father."

"Why not? You're the biggest threat, Thorne."

"I don't believe it."

"That, boy, is clear as daylight." Doc Zykin lets out a long breath. "And so I must kill you. Such a shame."

And with that, it's official. My luck really is crap.

Or maybe it isn't.

A plan forms. It's a last-ditch and desperate move, but it's all I have. My gaze locks on the closed door that separates me from Meimi.

What the hell. I'll try it.

Doc Zykin flips out a gash blade, just like the one Axel had on the mission with Emma. Zykin prowls toward me, I step back. Calling on my battle sentient, I summon body armor to cover my skin. Then I send my knowledge sentient out into the floor, just as I did before in the chemical plant. They lock right in on the hospital's data feed. I fish through information.

Patient intakes.

Budget numbers.

Parking lot assignments.

That's not what I need.

Doc Zykin swipes at my face. I dodge the blow and keep on the defensive.

"You're not attacking," says Doc Zykin slowly. "What are you scheming at?"

"How to stay alive," I reply.

A red fissure of light opens around the doctor. One moment, Zykin stands in front of me. The next, there's a surge of pain in my back. Twisting about, I see that the doctor has opened up a drift void to transport himself right behind me. I've never even heard of this kind of control before.

Reaching behind, I grasp at my lower back. The doc got a good swipe in there. The scent of burned rubber fills the air. It was more than a cut, all right. Those gash razors burn.

Every warrior sense in me wants to place all my focus on the battle sentient, but I stay the course. I need to find that program.

The Quantum Blocker Protocol.

I push my knowledge sentient far beyond the hospital's mainframe. At last, it finds a route to the city's software systems. Programs appears in my mind. There are ones for traffic light sensors. Sewer schematics. Power line fluctuation grids. School access codes.

Another flash of red light appears. Doc Zykin is back, and this time, he steps out of a red slash of brightness to stand right in front of me. Moving with supernatural speed, Zykin kicks my legs out from under me, sending me onto my back. He then pins me to the ground. Bringing his arm down, Zykin swings his gash razor closer to my throat. Lifting my arms, I block his attack. Still the super-heated metal blade sears my skin, even from a few inches away.

"What a shame I'll have to kill you," sneers Zykin. "But it's as your father said, one of us must die. And he didn't seem to care who lost their life, did he?" Doc presses forward until the blade brushes the skin at my throat. Searing pain burns along my neck.

Then it happens.

My knowledge sentient break into ECHO Academy and the software that's been allowing Doc Zykin to enter the Boston Dome in the first place. The Quantum Blocker Protocol. The system is still on its planned shut down, just as I saw last night.

Zykin presses his weapon lower. The blade cuts easily through my body armor, allowing the heated razor to bite into my skin. The tang of blood and charred flesh fills the air. It takes all my focus, but I keep on my original plan.

I order my vision sentient to create a drift void behind Doc Zykin. A loop of blue particles appears in the air up above Zykin's head. Soon it solidifies into what looks like a plate that's suspended in the air. A dark halo for an evil man.

My mind takes a snapshot of the moment. Now, I'm lying on my back with Doc Zykin pinning me to the floor. There's a solid drift void behind his head and a gash razor at my throat.

If my plan's going to work, now is my moment.

With all my focus, I order my battle sentient to give my arms strength. Power careens through my arms. With one great heave, I press upwards, shoving the doc high into the air. His head breaks through the drift void, smashing the blue plate into hundreds of tiny pieces. To my knowledge sentient, I then send a final command.

Restart the protocol.

Instantly, it happens. I lose all connection with my sentient as the quantum blocker kicks back into action. My drift void also disappears, but it does so with Doc Zykin's head in outer space and his body in Mass General. When the drift void disappears, Doc Zykin is decapitated. He falls over, dead.

With the Doc finally out of the picture, I rush over to the window and check on Meimi. The recovery room is empty. My transcendent is gone.

Damn.

CHAPTER 19

"There is no greater gift than finding your transcendent, and no tragedy more painful than losing them." – Empress Ophelia, *The Lost Book Of Transcendence*

FOR THE RECORD, it's a pain in the ass to clean up a decapitated body when you can't use ultra-high tech or your innate sentient superpowers. But I am in a hospital, so gurneys, disinfectant and a morgue are all rather easy to source. I even find some wound spray to hide the cuts in my back and neck. All in all, it's amazing what you can do in twenty minutes or less when you put your mind to it.

True story: the hardest part turns out to be dragging Nurse Oakes back onto his chair. The guy is heavier than he looks.

At last, my crime scene is as clean as it will get. Nurse Oakes is starting to make grumbling sounds. That guy will wake up soon. I enter my key card into one of the wall displays and search for Wisteria Roberts. There's a pause that seems to last an eternity before the monitor displays any info.

Wisteria Roberts
   Northwest Tower
   Fortieth floor
   Room 40562-B

I take off at a run. Turns out, Mass General has way too many towers in its complex. Eventually, I find the Northwest one. After an agonizing ride in a stainless steel elevator, I step out onto the fortieth floor. It's your typical hospital wing, if your hospital is a fancy hotel with stainless steel decorations.

Rounding a corner, I reach room 40562-B. A man stands outside wearing full black body armor. "Let me in!" He pounds on the door. "This is my charge!"

I know this fellow. In fact, I'm the one who got him caught for stealing government funds to ensure he had a high sperm count, among other things.

Captain Vargas.

I march up. "I'm her guard. You're relieved of duty."

A small bio-engineered animal paces by Vargas's feet. It's got a feline body with a bat's face and wings. From the files, I know the animal's name is Marrow, not that I'll let Vargas realize that fact.

"Let me see your ID," states Vargas.

I'm not handing him anything. I press the key card against a nearby data station that's set into the wall. The monitor brings up the image of my face, along with my title. I point to the words. "See what that says? Personal guard for Wisteria Roberts." I tap my chest. "That's me. You're excused."

Vargas still wear his full black helmet, but even with it on, I can see how the visor is steaming up inside. This must really be upsetting the guy.

"I must give her a wrist cuff," demands Vargas. "Humboldt wants her tracked."

"Take it up with Doc Godwin," I counter.

"I will."

With that, Vargas stomps off down the hallway. Marrow stalks closer to me and sniffs my boot. I smile. Marrow purrs and takes off. What can I say? I'm a cat guy. This may be a genetically altered breed, but whenever there is feline in the mix, that DNA always comes out on top. And felines always love Umbrans.

Once Vargas is gone, I turn to the door, set my key card against the entry pad, and wait.

With a soft click, the door opens.

Yes.

Inside the room, only a thin sliver of sunlight seeps through the shaded windows. I step inside and there she is. Meimi. My transcendent lays under her covers, her chest rising and falling in a steady rhythm.

Alive.

Safe.

Although her head is still bandaged, all the tubes are gone from her mouth and nose. It's a definite improvement. I scan the machines behind her. All her readouts look healthy, too.

At last, I'm here.

A drumroll of footsteps sounds behind me. It's Godwin. Today, he's in a lab coat complete with pocket protector.

"Good morning, Thorne."

I spin about to face him. "Hello, Sir."

"How do you like your charge?"

I shrug. "Not too much trouble."

"No one enters the room without my presence. Not even you. Just guard the door from the exterior. Keep everyone out."

"As you command."

Godwin beams. "We've big plans for her." Reaching into his pocket, Godwin pulls out another data stick. "You're to live in ECHO Academy. All the specifics are here." He hands me the stick. "And you'll find that your new chambers already contain more appropriate gear for your enhanced position." Godwin reaches up to pat my shoulder. He's rather shorter than I am, so he can only tap my lower bicep. Still, I appreciate the gesture.

"Congratulations," says Godwin.

"Thank you."

"Follow my instructions, that's all I ask. Anything else is a death wish."

I'm about to say, *thanks for the pep talk,* but I stop myself. Instead, I plaster on my most sincere smile. "Understood."

With that, my new employer turns and leaves. It doesn't seem to bother him that I haven't left the room, so I risk hanging behind. Once Godwin well and truly gone, I go over to Meimi's beside. She looks so beautiful in her sleep, even with her head bandages.

My transcendent.

Kneeling beside her, I take Meimi's hand in mine. Her warmth envelops more than my palm; my entire soul comes alive just to touch her again. A memory appears. Godwin wasn't the only one to warn me about death wishes. A few days and a million years ago, Justice said virtually the same thing. Back then, I lived to take risks. My limitations with sentient ate away at me like poison.

Not anymore.

Now, it no longer matters that I'm the weak prince. Instead, Meimi is what's important.

Footsteps sound in the outer hall. Even with the lights down, I can't risk lingering too close to Meimi, especially considering Godwin's warning about staying away. So I give her hand a gentle squeeze and step outside.

Closing the door, I lean against a nearby stretch of wall and keep watch. Doctors and nurses walk by. The occasional patient shuffles past in a hospital gown and slippers. It's the regular ebb and flow of a hospital. The same happens in most universes, I suppose. Somehow, it's all extraordinarily beautiful in my eyes, because this isn't just any hospital. It's the place where I'm keeping Meimi safe.

And no matter what, I will stay strong for her.

—The End—

The adventure continues with ALIEN MINDS, book 3 in the Dimension Drift. Read on for a sample chapter ...

ALIEN MINDS

The adventure continues with ALIEN MINDS, book 3 in the Dimension Drift ...

Try ANGELBOUND, the kick-ass paranormal romance with more than 1 million copies sold!

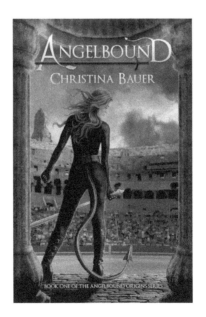

FAIRY TALES OF THE MAGICORUM

A modern fairy tale that *USA Today* calls a 'must-read!' Check out WOLVES AND ROSES!

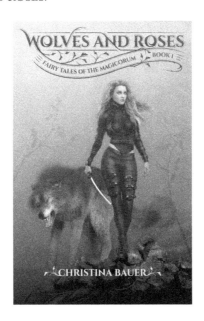

Medieval mages ... Slow-burn love ... And heart-pounding action! Check out the BEHOLDER series!

PIXIELAND DIARIES

PIXIELAND DIARIES tells the story of sassy pixie Calla and 'her' elf prince, Dare.

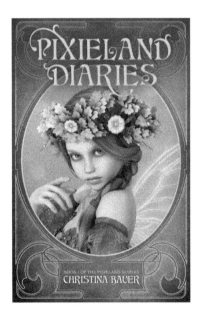

Meimi

IN THIS MOMENT, I know four things.

One, I just woke up in a hospital bed.

Two, I don't remember anything about my life before today. *Hello, amnesia!*

Three, I want out of here now because ...

Four, there's a creepy couple in my room—Luci and Josiah—who claim they're my sponsor parents. According to them, I'm a seventeen-year-old science prodigy called Wisteria Roberts.

Huh. That name rings zero bells.

Plus, these two make my skin crawl.

"We sponsor you *financially*," explains Josiah. "Then in the fall, we'll fund your senior year of high school at ECHO Academy." Josiah's a lanky guy with slicked-back hair, a frayed suit, and an overly large Adam's apple.

"Afterward, you'll pay us back with interest," adds Luci. "Forty percent. Compounded annually."

Luci is tall and willowy with white-blonde tresses. By contrast, I'm a curvy girl with brown hair and ebony eyes. I'm also wrapped up mummy-style with bandages. According to Luci and Josiah, I took a spill on Newbury Street and lost my memory. So sketchy.

Some small voice in my head cries that I should be terrified right now. Instead, I just feel numb. Must be a happy side effect of having no memory. Like an amnesia bonus.

"You'll love living in our dorm," says Josiah. "In fact, think of me more as your sponsor *friend* than your sponsor *parent*."

At this point, that small part of me screams how Josiah is a disgusting pig. But more of me is still happily numb, so the warnings go nowhere.

Screech, screech, screech!

A chorus of alarm bells sound. Red lights flash in the outer hallway. An overly calm female voice drones through hidden speakers. "Cleansing search commencing ... cleansing search commencing. All hail the Authority ... All hail the Authority."

With that, the inner cogs of my brain connect and whir. Feelings return. My blood chills over with fear. I may not recall my personal history, but I do remember how our evil government—what we call the Authority—conducts cleansing searches. They find the sick or poor, label them as *undesirable,* and slate them for *cleansing.* It's a fancy word for murder.

The alarms wail louder. My heart rate skyrockets. If there's a cleansing search, I'm a slam dunk to be undesirable.

A cat-like animal slinks into the room. My eyes almost bulge out of my head. This is one of the Horde, which are genetically altered attack animals. In this case, the creature has a feline body paired with the hide of a serpent and bat wings. A golden collar encircles its throat. The creature sniffs at me once before letting out a high-pitched howl.

Yee-oooow!

I grip my sheets and shiver. At this point, I'm only inches away from death. The way that cat-snake-bat yowls, the animal is calling for its master.

Sure enough, a warrior bursts through the door. He wears black body armor that's patterned with charred-out bones and paired with a skull-like helmet. I know that particular uniform. This guy is one of the Merciless, warriors who specialize in cleansings.

I'm so dead. Literally.

"I'm Captain Vargas." The Merciless gestures toward the cat-snake-bat. "This is Marro." He then points straight at my nose. "My animal called me here because it scents you as undesirable."

Bolts of worry move through my torso. This is not good news.

Vargas lifts a gash gun from the holster at his waistline. "Prepare to be cleansed."

I look over to Luci and Josiah. In response to the threat to their supposed *sponsor child*, they gasp, pale, and retreat to a far corner. *Thanks for nothing.*

Closing my eyes, I wait for the inevitable.

No blast sounds.

Instead, the alarms fall silent. Reopening my eyes, I see a wisp of a man stroll into the room. Tufts of gray hair encircle his balding head. Small round glasses sit atop his thin nose. The name tag on his loose lab coat reads *Dr. Godwin*.

My heart sinks.

Yup, it's *that* Dr. Godwin, the guy who runs the attack Horde, of which Marro is only one example.

Things keep getting better and better.

Although Godwin stands far shorter than Vargas, the doctor swaggers toward the towering warrior.

"What are you doing here?" snaps Godwin.

"Routine visit," replies Vargas.

"Then why are you holding your gash gun?" asks Godwin.

Vargas quickly reholsters his weapon. "No reason."

I raise my hand. After all, Godwin looks on my side here. "He was totally about to cleanse me," I state.

Godwin frowns. "We've been through this a hundred times, Vargas. You are forbidden from killing my patients."

My eyes almost bug out of my head. *I'm Godwin's patient?* Luci and Josiah said I'd gotten in an accident, but not *who* was treating my memory loss. Godwin's on the government's Star Council, which means he's the nastiest of the nasties. Having him as my doctor will not end well.

"Did your animal bite her?" asks Godwin.

"Not yet," replies Vargas.

"Good. Be sure to keep your beast away from my patient." Godwin glares at Vargas. "And don't *you* go near her again, either."

For the record, I like the direction this conversation is taking. *Not being killed by Vargas* is a good plan, even if it does come from Godwin.

"Near or not, I'll keep tabs on her." Vargas pulls out a metal cuff from somewhere. A second later, he snaps the device on my wrist. Cool steel presses against my skin. I have to hand it to Vargas—the guy moves pretty quickly for a massive dude in heavy black armor.

Still gripping my forearm, Vargas lifts my wrist up for a closer examination. For the first time, I notice a small screen embedded into the metal. The display reads: *Wisteria Roberts, private staff for Dr. Godwin, goal loading in process.*

I try yanking my arm free from Vargas's hold. The guy's grip is like iron.

"I didn't give permission for that," snarls Godwin.

Vargas folds his arms over his chest. "Everyone gets a wrist cuff, even if they're a legitimate citizen. If you don't like it, take it up with

Humboldt." General Humboldt runs the Merciless; Dr. Godwin leads the Horde of genetically enhanced killer creatures. The two have a hate-hate relationship.

Turning away from Godwin, Vargas focuses on me once more. "Now I can track your every move," he explains.

"Oh." That numb feeling returns. It's like I'm a mindless pawn on a chessboard—no idea what the real players are doing. I find myself staring at the cuff. "This says something about goals."

"Soon you'll receive updates on the Liberation Celebration." Vargas sighs, as if simply saying the words Liberation Celebration were some kind of prayer.

His attitude is not a shocker. Every August, the Liberation Celebration commemorates the day the Authority took power. It's a huge deal.

"This year, we're adding a contest to the event," adds Vargas. "It's between the Merciless and the Horde." Vargas nods in the doctor's direction. "Godwin's side is losing."

"Leave," orders Godwin.

Vargas winks. "As you command."

With that, Vargas marches off down the outer hallway. Marro slinks along behind him, the little creature's bat wings fluttering with each step. Poor Marro. If that golden collar were off, then he'd probably scamper away to chase mice. Horde animals aren't naturally mean.

"Impossible man." Godwin steps back to my bedside. As the doctor moves closer, my skin prickles with fear. This doctor is familiar. Although I can't remember where we met or anything, I know one fact.

Godwin is a dick and I hate him.

"It's true that I'm behind in terms of the competition," continues Godwin. "But in order to take the lead, I need top scientists. You're supposedly a prodigy, so I've spent weeks rescuing your mind. Now you owe me everything. Will you help me win?"

I pretend to consider this before replying. "It's tempting, but no thanks. Just send me back to where I came from, and I'll be fine."

Under the bedsheets, I cross my fingers. *Please send me back.*

Godwin points toward Luci and Josiah. "You met your sponsor parents. Don't you want to live in safety and comfort while attending ECHO Academy, the world's greatest school for science? In return, all you need do is provide a little assistance for the celebration. Swear to help me and it's all yours."

I wince a bit, like I'm seriously thinking this through once more. "Nope. Still not interested. I'm just—" I pat my head bandages "—recovering from brain surgery and everything."

Godwin rounds on Luci and Josiah. "You two. Out."

"What do you mean?" Josiah's mouth falls open. "Wisteria's not our sponsor child anymore?"

Godwin's thin nostrils flare with rage. "Wisteria will stay under my personal care. If I have need of you, I'll let you know."

Luci slumps. "But I thought—"

"Go!" orders Godwin.

In another display of fake-parent awesomeness, Luci and Josiah skitter from the room. A pang of disappointment fills my soul. It's as if I knew Luci and Josiah, but expected more from them.

A sneaky look lights up Godwin's bland face. "Since you aren't willing to help, I must resort to more brutal motivations. I've found a private guard for you." He snaps his fingers. "Enter."

A boy stalks into the room. Wearing fitted black body armor, the guard looks about eighteen years old with broad shoulders and a lean, muscular body. His hair is cut short—military style—and sets off the heavy angles of his face. But what stuns me are his eyes.

Large.

Blue.

Soulful.

My breath catches. *I definitely know this boy. He's important.* Every cell in my body wants to remember more. Stupid amnesia.

Godwin sets his hand on the guy's shoulder. "Introduce yourself."

If the boy recognizes me, he doesn't show it. His eyes stay cold as his gaze locks with mine. "I'm Thorne Oxblood."

My throat tightens with grief. I don't remember this guy, so why does this moment feel like such a betrayal? After all, I handled waking up with amnesia no problem. I sailed past the *Luci and Josiah Show* like some part of me was expecting it.

But Thorne? His empty stare hits me like a body blow. Despite my best efforts, a whimper escapes my lips. *This is horrible.*

I glance over to Godwin. The word *smug* pretty much sums up the doctor's face. "Now, that's more the reaction I was expecting." Godwin focuses on Thorne. "Tell her what I've hired you to do."

"I'm here to ensure your compliance," states Thorne. "Dr. Godwin requires your unique services to meet his goals for the Liberation Celebration. You will help him or die."

All my sass melts through the floor. Something about Thorne tears at my soul in a deeper way than anything from Godwin, Luci, or Josiah.

This can't be happening.

Once more, Godwin claps his hand on Thorne's shoulder. "Make sure the girl's ready for testing first thing tomorrow morning. I must confirm her skills before moving forward."

Thorne stiffens his stance. "Yes, sir."

"Did you say *testing?*" I sit up straighter. "Don't I need more time to recover?"

"Let me clarify a few things." Godwin's voice transforms into a sinister whisper. "I don't want your help. If I weren't so desperate for scientists, I wouldn't even consider you. And if you're any good, you'll become nothing but a whisper and a shadow. Every success you achieve will be attributed to me. I trust we understand each other."

Without waiting for a reply, Godwin presses a button on the wall. "Knock her out."

A young woman's voice sounds from hidden speakers. "Yes, Dr. Godwin."

Blue fluid fills my IV tube. I frown. That particular shade of drug is familiar.

Tranquilizer.

In this moment, one thing becomes clear. *I'll never help Godwin win at the Liberation Celebration.* In fact, I'd love to explode the whole thing in his smarmy face.

Within seconds, my eyelids droop. A low whir sounds as the blinds auto-close on my bay windows. Godwin takes off. The door shuts behind him with a soft click, leaving me in shadows.

Thorne stands against the wall, silent and staring. He could be the cover boy for *Cruel Killer* magazine, the guy's so intimidating.

As my consciousness fades, I focus on my wrist cuff. Words flash in a dim green glow.

Update Complete
Star Council Level Access: Godwin
Humboldt-Merciless Undesirables Tagged: 1,342,109
Godwin-Horde Undesirables Tagged: 443,808
Total To Be Announced At Liberation Celebration: 1,785,917

What in the ever-loving Darwin?

That's what this is all about?

According to this readout, Godwin and Humboldt are racing to tag the most undesirables for death ... with their grand totals to be broadcast at the Liberation Celebration. A sick taste crawls up my throat. President Hope has made a game from marking people for execution.

Maybe I don't know who I am, but I must have family somewhere. A word appears in my mind: *mother*. I don't know my mom's name or where she is, but I feel certain of one fact. My mother's an undesirable. To keep her safe, I must help the others as well. As my consciousness fades, my thoughts reel through options.

An idea appears.

Perhaps I can put Godwin in jail, escape this scary scene, ruin the Liberation Celebration, and save every undesirable—including my mother—all at once.

I just need a *team*.

As my eyes flutter closed, I notice how Thorne watches me with extra interest. Now that Godwin's gone, my badass guard looks all things wide-eyed and sweet.

That settles it.

He'll be my first team recruit.

Thorne

"Intoxication with technology is the hallmark of an underdeveloped society." – Beauregard the Great, *Instructions for Visiting Parallel Worlds*

After spending hours on guard duty, I can finally leave Mass General. Soon I'm tooling my hoverbike toward the outskirts of the Boston Dome. Overhead, a cloud-free sky is projected onto the plasma. Tall buildings loom around me in a maze of chrome, concrete, and blinking lights.

An image appears in my mind. Meimi—I never even *think* the false name Wisteria—lies curled on her hospital bed, drugged up and asleep. Every instinct in my soul says I should've stayed behind and guarded her while she rested. Not an option. An important appointment is coming up, and I can't miss it.

For Meimi.

Of course, Godwin doesn't know I'm leaving the city. Then again, the doctor doesn't know a lot of things about me.

Like the fact that I'm not from this planet.

Plus, I'm not just any alien. My father's the Emperor of the Omni-verse, the universe of universes.

So what Godwin doesn't know about me is quite a lot, actually.

Glancing down, I check my smart watch. Based on the time,

Godwin's still off chatting with President Hope. Those meetings last for hours. I'm good to leave the dome until dawn.

At the foot of Mass Avenue, I reach a line of arches set into the dome's glassy base. *Checkpoint Seven.* Electric cars, regular pedal bikes, and hoverbuses—all of them wait in long lines under the archways. One aisle always stays empty, though. It's reserved for Star Council members and their adjuncts, like me. I pull up there.

A Merciless warrior steps out. He's dressed head to toe in black armor with a helmet shaped to resemble a skull. A small attack animal creeps along at the fighter's side: a cat with reptile skin and bat wings. Only one guy keeps that particular attack animal handy. I stifle a groan.

Captain Vargas. He's found me. Again.

Vargas works for General Humboldt, a bigwig who loathes Godwin. Together, Humboldt and Godwin are both trying to undermine President Hope.

It's a really twisted situation.

Peeling off his helmet, Vargas marches over to my hoverbike. Like all Merciless, Vargas is in his late twenties, pale skinned, golden haired, and handsome. He's also been screened for certain psychological profile: no empathy, high intellect, and strong predatory instinct.

In other words, a successful sociopath.

Vargas flashes me a winning smile. "Lovely day. Eh, Thorne?"

No one's more charming than a sociopath. Best to keep every conversation to a minimum. "What do you want, Vargas?"

"Why so hostile?" He widens his eyes in the perfect replication of surprise. What the guy really feels is nothing. That is, unless he's attacking someone.

"Because you're tracking me when you should be tagging undesirables."

All traces of a smile vanish. Vargas doesn't bother to deny that Humboldt has him trailing me. "I could slap a wrist cuff on you."

"I'm an adjunct member of the Star Council. My boss has his own way of keeping tabs on me."

As a matter of fact, Godwin injected a DNA tracker directly into my bloodstream. I overrode it, though. Right now, those markers show I'm in Meimi's room. The only way Godwin would think otherwise is if he stopped by the hospital. And since the doctor's in with President Hope, he won't.

"Try again," I tell Vargas.

"According to data feeds, you should be at Mass General, looking over

Godwin's *patient*." The way Vargas says *patient*, I know he suspects Meimi is something more. *Not good.*

"So?"

"Why are you leaving the city?" asks Vargas.

"Want my plans? You know the protocol. Ask Godwin."

Vargas chuckles. "I already know what you're up to. You've a suite reserved at the Berkshire Mini-Dome and Deluxe Resort. It's only a short ride from the city. Exclusive. Romantic. Perfect for a certain lady, eh?"

Whenever I leave the Boston Dome, I always set up a reservation at the Berkshire Resort, just in case I need an alibi. Vargas thinks he caught me sneaking off for a woman. Instead, he's only becoming part of my cover-up.

When I answer, I take care to keep my face blank. "Wave me on, Vargas."

"Not a chance. Godwin ordered you back to Mass Gen."

I check my smart watch. There are zero texts from Godwin. Vargas is bluffing. This guy has no idea where I'm supposed to be or why. This is how sociopaths pass the time—playing mind games with the rest of us.

Or in this case, *trying* to play mind games.

I lower my voice. "Let. Me. Through."

There's a long moment where Vargas stares at me. His hands ball into fists, a movement that makes his armor crackle. It's an invitation to fight.

Every cell in my body wants to battle this guy.

Or since I'm from Umbra, it's more accurate to say every *sentient* does.

My people are unique because our bodies store sentient, the most powerful beings in the omniverse. Sentient may look like particles, but they're actually tiny cybernetic organisms that work as a hive mind to give us extra powers, like battle energy. Right now, my battle sentient are screaming for me to smash Vargas in the face. They communicate by sending me images of my fist crushing the warrior's nose.

And because I'm adjunct to the Star Council, I could get away with it too.

On reflex, I start the process of activating my sentient. I picture tiny black particles seeping out from under my skin, covering my body in heavy armor. Next, I imagine more lacing through my muscles to provide extra strength. The sentient stir inside me, but they don't appear.

My back teeth lock in frustration. For some reason, the Boston Dome blocks sentient from departing my body. It's infuriating. It's also why I must leave for this chat with my brothers. Normally, I'd just summon my knowledge sentient to contact them. But because of the dome, I must exit the city and connect at a specific time. All of which adds up to one thing.

If I want to take Vargas down, I'll have to do it human style.

Which wouldn't be too hard, actually.

In fact, a fistfight might let off some steam.

I kill the engine on my hoverbike. "Give me an excuse."

Vargas pauses for another long second, and then waves me on. "Fine. Go."

A little disappointing, that.

When it comes to battle, humans are no match for an Umbran like me. Even so, since Vargas has all that armor, he might have been interesting. I could have even freed Marro when I was done.

Ah, well. Another time.

Revving up my hoverbike, I take off at top speed through the dome wall. The moment I'm through, the road changes from smooth concrete into cracked asphalt. Gray skies loom overhead, filled with green-tinted rainclouds. In every direction, the landscape is nothing but rubble. The scent of rotten eggs fills the air.

Leaving the dome by hoverbike isn't a common choice. Most people prefer a fully enclosed vehicle. That way, you avoid breathing unfiltered air. And sure enough, bits of soot, grime, and other gunk float before my eyes. I swear, there are coal mines with better atmospheres than Reformed New England.

But since I'm out of the dome, I can easily fix the air-quality problem.

Finally, I contact my sentient again.

Fast as a heartbeat, I send them a mental image of an air-screening mask, goggles, and an earpiece. This time, my sentient respond instantly. Silver particles rise from my skin, quickly forming the shapes needed.

After that, my sentient send me a mental image of a man punching his fist high. That's their way of saying it's good to be useful once more.

"Missed me?" I ask.

In reply, the mental image turns into a crowd cheering.

"Yeah, missed you too."

I don't store a lot of sentient, but the ones I have? After years of training, I've gained close control over every particle.

For the next hour, I speed over broken roads. Eventually I reach the ruins of an old apartment complex. The spot reminds me of a doll house: an entire wall has been sheared off, revealing sixteen floors of people's lives the moment before the Authority took them down. There's a living room with a faded-pink couch that hangs over the ledge, a library with books strewn across the floor, and a nursery with a toppled-over crib. *Sad, really.*

Parking my hoverbike, I march up to the building's front door and step inside the lobby. It's pretty standard stuff for old Earth. There's a reception desk, now smashed. A wall of mailboxes stand nearby; they're also demolished. Yellowing envelopes and faded catalogs still sit in exposed boxes. Some couches litter the floor, all of them covered in mold and collapsing in on themselves. Greenish dust covers everything. In the twenty years since the Authority attacked, few people have stepped in this place... which makes it the perfect spot to meet my brothers, Justice and Slate.

Still, the building sets my nerves on edge. It's too much like a cemetery. Out of habit, I peel off my human covering, allowing my sentient to come out and take their place. Within seconds, I'm wearing black body armor that's indestructible and made from sentient. No self-respecting Umbran meets his people in human clothes.

My earpiece beeps as Justice calls.

"Accept comm," I say.

"Slate and I are coming through." Even though he's universes away, Justice's deep baritone sounds perfectly clear. That's all the work of his sentient. Like me, Justice and Slate also command these cybernetic organisms.

"Check that," I reply.

My heart lightens. It'll be good to see my brothers again.

A hoop of silver particles appears in the air before me. It's the beginnings of a drift void, which is how we travel between universes. Since this circle is silver, the void's created by knowledge sentient. There are four kinds of sentient in all: black for battle, silver for knowledge, blue for second sight (meaning visions of the present or future), and red for danger.

The particles spin in heavier loops until the center transforms into a solid circle of gray. The sight reminds me of a silver plate hanging in midair.

Then Justice punches through.

From the other side of the drift void, my brother strikes. Justice's fist smashes through the center of the void, opening a portal between this version of Earth and my home world of Umbra. Justice steps through the round opening between our realities.

My older brother cuts a bulky figure in his long duster, heavy boots, and scarred face. Basically, he's a younger version of our father, Cole.

Both are the perfect combination of intellect and a hefty right hook. Justice is a master of battle sentient, second only to the Emperor himself.

A moment later, Slate slips past the round portal. My younger brother is a tall and sinewy with a long face and shoulder-length white hair. As a master of second sight sentient, Slate wears a deep indigo jacket with a high collar and straight cut. Not for the first time, my brothers remind me of a cowboy and preacher from Umbra's Wild West days.

Or maybe it's Earth's Wild West days. So hard to tell. My family *guards and gardens the omniverse*, meaning that we encourage certain lines of parallel universes to expand while others die out. Over the millennia, it gets easy to mix up *what* comes from *where,* if that makes sense.

With Slate through the drift void, the portal spirals into smaller circles. Within seconds, the connection has completely disappeared.

Justice grins. His symmetrical smile highlights his rugged, twice-broken nose. "Thorne. Good to see you." He sets his hand on my neck. "I still can't believe it. A transcendent."

I grin. He means Meimi, of course.

A transcendent is someone you love deeply across so many parallel universes, that connection bleeds over into your current reality. We were raised that the very idea of a transcendent is a fairy tale.

Even so, it's true.

Meimi is my transcendent.

It still doesn't seem possible.

Since I command few sentient, I'm the weak brother. The extra prince. An unworthy guy who got a free pass to the royal table. If anyone found a transcendent, it should have been Justice. He's the one who'll someday become Emperor. How I ended up deserving an honor such as Meimi, I'll never understand.

I only know that I'll protect her with everything I am.

Justice leans over until our foreheads gently touch. There's no mistaking the deep smile in his voice as he speaks. "Transcendents exist. What a boon."

"Don't forget," I counter. "Meimi and I are *soul* transcendents. She's not Umbran. We only share thoughts and feelings, not sentient power."

Justice shrugs and steps back. "I'd take that. You're a lucky man."

My smile widens. *I am indeed.*

Standing ramrod straight, Slate grips his fists behind his back. "Explain," he declares. My younger brother's voice is resonant and, as always, only heard for a word or two. By saying *explain*, that's Slate's way of asking for full details on me and Meimi.

My little brother doesn't chatter much. I figure it's because he lives in multiple futures with his second sight sentient. Or it could be that he's the baby of the family, so he got used to me and Justice doing all the talking.

"Let me think." I pause, trying to recall the last time I spoke with my brothers. "I saw you right after Meimi was taken by Godwin." It's only been a matter of weeks, but it feels like years have passed since then. "Since that day, there hasn't been much to tell. Godwin erased Meimi's memory, just like I expected." The very thought heats my blood with fury.

No one should have touched a hair on Meimi's head, let alone erased her memory.

Still, I can be thankful I saw it coming and could do something about it. Blinking hard, I refocus on my brothers.

"Meimi's been unconscious in hospitals most of the time," I continue. "I wheedled my way into Godwin's confidence so I could watch over her. Now I'm her guard."

"What about her—?" Justice taps his temple.

"Before Godwin took Meimi, I was able to link with her mind and leverage my own second sight sentient. They're keeping her memories safe." I don't add in the part about having to kiss her to get the job done. My brothers know how blue sentient work. And my kisses are nobody else's business.

Slate frowns. Since his face is all high cheek bones and smooth lines, that grimace is like breaking up a sculpture. "Meet," he says again. That means he wants details from before Godwin entered the picture.

My brows lift. This is a lot of talking from Slate. And frowning? It's an avalanche of emotion.

"All right." I hold my hands up, palms forward. "When I first saw Meimi, our minds instantly connected. There was no push from my sentient. It just ... happened. I could feel her emotions; she sensed mine as well. And we both received visions of the future—of us dancing, riding hoverbikes, that kind of stuff." My heart warms just remembering the experience.

"Were you shocked?" asks Justice. Normally, I'd give him guff about all these questions about feelings. After all, Justice is a big bad warrior. But my older brother seems so genuinely concerned, I can't make any jokes.

His interest is cool.

More than that, actually.

It's sweet.

And for a rough warrior like Justice, that's a big deal.

"Oh, I was floored when the visions first came in," I reply. "But the whole thing became more overwhelming for Meimi, so I shut down our link. I only opened it up once more to save her memories. And since then, nothing like that connection has happened again." I scratch my cheek and wince. "I'm pretty sure she hates me now that she's awake. Not that I blame her. Godwin presented me as her badass guard."

"You can't give her back her memories?" asks Justice.

"Kiss," says Slate.

And there it is. They both know how it works.

"Not yet." Frustration tightens across my neck and shoulders. "My powers are blocked while I'm under the Boston Dome. No kissing—no activating her memories—until I get her out of Boston. Not that there's been a chance to help her leave. Until today, Meimi's been unconscious and in the middle of different *procedures from Godwin*." There's no hiding the acid in my tone as I say that last bit. "But she's recovered and mobile now. I'll get her out soon."

"Override," declares Slate.

I look to Justice. "What does he mean?"

"Slate's seen some futures where you override that block. We're working on options."

"Thanks." This is good news. Umbran tech is far more advanced than Earthen. In fact, I'm amazed that humans came up with anything that could block our sentient in the first place.

Now that we've covered the happy subject—namely Meimi—it's time to cover darker topics.

"How's Cole?" I ask.

That's our father, Emperor of the Omniverse. To become ruler, Cole had to take in a ton of Crown Sentient, a super-powerful breed of these cybernetic nanocreatures. Crown Sentient allow my father to see multiple universes and dimensions, but they're also eating away at his mind.

"Cole's still Cole," says Justice. "The emperor's obsessed that I have a transcendent. Thinks it's the end of his rule."

My chest tightens with worry. When our father is sane, we call him Dad. When he's not, then his name's Cole. Sadly, he's been Cole more and more lately.

"Sorry you had to deal with that alone." I tap my earpiece. "Wish I could contact you when I'm in the dome."

"Not to worry." Justice adjusts his white Stetson. "Take care of your transcendent. Let Slate and I handle Cole."

Slate's gray eyes widen. "Coming."

"You mean Cole?" I ask.

Slate nods. My heart sinks. My father is following us here.

No, not my father. *Cole.*

And he's been obsessing over transcendents.

There's not much I can do to protect Meimi from him, considering how weak I am with sentient. Even so, what I lack in sentient power, I make up for in training, learning, and determination.

I can only hope this time, that's enough to save Meimi.

———

—End Of Sample—

Order ALIEN MINDS, book 3 in the Dimension Drift!

NEW APPENDIX OF TOTALLY AWESOME GOODIES

INTRODUCTION

WELCOME TO THIS NEW APPENDIX!

I've added lots of extra stuff here in order to celebrate the release of new covers for my Dimension Drift series! Check them out below:

Say it with me: *ooooh, aaaaaah!*

Now, you may wonder: *what's behind the new covers?*
Good question, you.
There are my five reasons why I did this.

One. The 'I Gotta Be Me' Cover

With the original covers, the first three had a theme of characters running through walls. Then the fourth book, ECHO ACADEMY, did it own thing. It was walls, walls, walls and... WTF? That bugged me.

Two. I Like Visuals

Reviewers often say that reading my books is like watching a movie in their heads. And hey, that's what it's like when I write them, too! Even after the books are launched, I'm still picturing the story and how to enhance it. All of which leads to item number three...

Three. More Books A-Coming

Great news! I plan on adding two more books to the series, namely JUSTICE and SLATE. As it was before, the cover design template wasn't really expandable to those guys. After all, you can only run through so many walls before things starts to get repetitive. This new format will fit in the two new titles perfectly. Yay!

Four. Getting Less Literal

The first covers represented actual scenes from the books. It was fun at the time, but I think it's a little limiting in the long run. Plus, this series is science fiction which I think lends itself to more *suggestive versus literal* design. The new look should give you an idea of the book's themes without getting too specific.

Four. Reader Goodies

Recently, I added an extra appendix to SLIPPERS AND THIEVES, a title from my Fairy Tales of the Magicorum series. Readers really liked it—and I love making you all happy—so the new covers were a good excuse to add in more content here as well.

All in all, I truly hope you enjoy these extra goodies... and please keep an eye out for a release date on JUSTICE and SLATE!

Best,
Christina Bauer, Author

THORNE IS one of my all-time favorite characters to write. Here are the three biggest drivers behind his personality!

Factor Number Three.
A Prince Of No Consequence

The biggest factor driving Thorne is that his entire family have power over sentient. These are minute cybernetic organisms that look like tiny particles. Sentient live inside a host's body and give them quantum abilities (think high-tech magic). Basically, intergalactic royalty in this book need sentient magic to be taken seriously, and Thorne has little sentient power. As a result, he's treated like an unworthy royal. Thorne takes huge risks to prove that he still has value. Basically, our guy has got a bit of a death wish when the book opens.

Factor Number Two.
Putting the Fun in DysFUNctional Family

What do you do when someone you love acts in the wrong ways ... but for all the right reasons? Thorne's father became Emperor of the Omniverse because the previous ruler was committing mass genocide. But the job of Emperor means taking in Crown Sentient, and those eat away at your mind. Thorne and his brothers try to make the best of a tough situation, but it isn't easy to watch a parent lose themselves. This also contributes to Thorne's risk-taking behavior (see factor number three).

Factor Number One.
Love Supports Life

Thorne then meets a lady who loves him (can't say more without spoilers) and that changes everything. He realizes that if he has enough value to inspire love from someone else, then maybe he should try liking himself as well. UMBRA is written in Thorne's voice, and it was very satisfying to write from a guy's perspective about the transformative power of love.

So there you have it; three factors that drive the character of Thorne. I can't wait to revisit him in the upcoming books, JUSTICE and SLATE!

MY WRITING PROCESS

FOLKS OFTEN ASK me about my writing process. After thirty books, I've racked up a few tips and tricks. Here's my biggest revelation...

It's Okay To Suck At Writing.
Seriously.

Here's the deal. Want to be a writer someday? Then have I got news for you: believe it or not, it's okay to suck at writing. Really. And for the record, I'm not talking about 'wow that paragraph could maybe get reworked' suck. I'm talking serious, top-of-the-line, vacuum-cleaner-that-picks-up-bowling-balls-level of suckage, and for a really-really-really long time.

And no, I am not kidding.

In fact, such awfulness is typical and, if handled properly, a sign of great things to come.

Still not kidding.

Here's my story on this subject. I didn't speak until about five, but once I started, I loved to tell stories about the worlds in my head. My first was an elaborate multi-generational quest set in a world inspired by the game Candyland (the bad guy lived in a chocolate palace). Soon, I was sharing these stories at school---during class, unsolicited---to the point where the nuns had to set aside 'special story time' for me so I'd shut up for most of the day (yeah, I was *that* kid). Once I got the knack of writing, I compulsively penned my tales instead, much to the nun's joy. Later, when it I hit upper grade school, English class was my personal bitch.

Oh, how I thought I rocked.

And lo, Freshman year of High School arrived. With it came more nuns and my first big-girl High School English paper. Man, I worked hard on that sucker. I handed it in and waited with baited breath for the inevitable 100 to come back, the page littered with side notes on my awesomeness. Sure enough, the paper came back, but not with a 100 on the top.

I got a 67. Not a total failure, but pretty darned close. Whoa.

'Devastated' pretty much describes my reaction to this 67. My life was predicated on the concept that I rocked at writing. Now, this seemed no longer true. Even worse, there were kids in my very same class that got perfect 100's on their first paper. Holy shit. They were better than I was. At. Writing.

This launched some major soul searching. I debated about never writing again, for reals. I felt mightily crushed and lied to...what were all those accolades in years gone by? What silly, torturous games were the nuns playing with me in grade school? This mope-fest went on until I eventually pulled up my big girl panties and went back at it, working hard for a better grade. This was Freshman year. I didn't get a 100 on a writing essay until I hit Senior year of English. So there you go.

When I got to college, I had no problems getting good grades, but there were other shocks in store. I met some other writers who were so freaking amazing, it made me want to drop writing again. For example, one kid I met Freshman year wrote his essays in iambic pentameter because, well, he was bored. Bored, I tell you! And it was goooooooood stuff. Like, I could work for weeks and not come up with two lines that were half as lovely. I don't know where that kid is now, but I wouldn't be surprised if he hit his own version of a '67' at some point, just like I did, and had to face the question: now that I have to work my ass off for this, is this still worth it?

Now, the 'worth it' conundrum isn't really a question anyone can answer *for you*, especially when it comes to writing. That said, at the time, I think it might've helped moi to know that the cycle of sucking-to-getting-better is pretty typical. In fact, it's a sign that your work is growing, and that's not just okay, that's amazing.

Today, I sincerely hope that every book I write kicks the ass of my last one.

Because, at the end of the day, that kind of suck is awesome.

TOP FANTASY BOOKS WITH KICK-ASS HEROINES

WHERE DO I get my inspiration for writing kick-ass heroines? Here are five of my favorite sources.

Five.
The Lord of the Rings by J R R Tolkien

If you want the original chick-power story in fantasy, then J R R Tolkien is the bomb. What he lacks in *quantity* of badass heroines, the guy more than makes up for in *quality*. Galadriel alone is worth the price of the book.

Four.
Grimm's Fairy Tales by the Brother's Grimm

My first entrance to fantasy was through the original *Grimm's Fairy Tales*. Now, I'm not referring to the sanitized Disney version, although I enjoyed those as well. I'm talking the gritty stuff where Snow White ends up dead. These stories were recorded by the brother's Grimm, but the tales themselves were created by women. Reading these stories as an adult, you can picture these wonderful ladies and the wisdom they were trying to convey. A must-read!

Three.

Mythology by Edith Hamilton

Another treasure-trove of badass females may be found in this compendium of Greco-Roman myths written in the style of Grimm's Fairy Tales. Such an eye opener in terms of truly great female leaders, from Hera to Athena.

Two.
The Egyptian Story of Isis

I read this one for a decade—in multiple translations—before I truly understood it. Isis was the original goddess story and her tale stretches back in use at least 40,000 years. It's a story of power, sacrifice and intellect. But don't go out and hunt down translations like I did; you can get the short version by checking out my blog post on the subject.

One.
Throne of Glass by Sarah J Maas

If you want to experience kick-ass chicks in modern literature, then this series by Sarah J Maas is one you cannot miss! Maas says she was inspired to write the books by the mental image of Cinderella at the ball with a knife hidden in her gown. What's not to love?

So there you have it—five of my favorite inspirations for chicks who kick ass and take names.

STANDARD APPENDIX OF STUFF
THAT'S STILL PRETTY COOL

IF YOU ENJOYED THIS BOOK...

...Please consider leaving a review, even if it's just a line or two. Every bit truly helps.

Plus I have it on good authority that every time you review an indie author, somewhere an angel gets a mocha latte.

For reals.

And angels need their caffeine, too.

ACKNOWLEDGMENTS

If you're reading my freaking acknowledgements, chances are, I should thank you for something. So, for the record: you are awesome, dear reader.

That said, huge and heartfelt thanks must go out to my husband and son for their rock-solid support. Being an author means a lot of early mornings, late nights, long weekends, and never-ending patience. You two are the best guys in the universe, period.

After that, I must thank the extensive network of reviewers, friends and colleagues who helped me build my writing chops in general. Gracias.

Finally, deep affection goes out to my late, much loved, and dearly missed Aunt Sandy and Uncle Henry. You saw the writer in me, always. Thank you, first and last.

ABOUT CHRISTINA BAUER

Christina Bauer thinks that fantasy books are like bacon: they just make life better. All of which is why she writes romance novels that feature demons, dragons, wizards, witches, elves, elementals, and a bunch of random stuff that she brainstorms while riding the Boston T. Oh, and she includes lots of humor and kick-ass chicks, too. Christina lives in Newton, MA with her husband, son, and semi-insane golden retriever, Ruby.

Stalk Christina on Social Media

Blog:
http://monsterhousebooks.com/blog/category/christina

Facebook:
https://www.facebook.com/authorBauer/

Instagram:
https://www.instagram.com/christina_cb_bauer/

Twitter:
@CB_Bauer

VLOG:
https://tinyurl.com/Vlogbauer

Web site:
www.bauersbooks.com

COMPLIMENTARY BOOK

Get a FREE book when you sign up for Christina's newsletter: https://tinyurl.com/bauersbooks

CPSIA information can be obtained
at www.ICGtesting.com
Printed in the USA
LVHW111156090821
694847LV00010B/1359